DI
Za

www.zachbohannon.com

Edited and Proofread by:
Jennifer Collins

Cover design by Johnny Digges
www.diggescreative.com

PROLOGUE

Dylan

A certain aura of fear and hateful lust filled the air. It held the hand of a musty stench, consuming the space they were in. The girls shuddered, and the preacher babbled on. And the boy, by no choice of his own, remained silent, made so by the dirty sock that gagged him.

It hadn't taken his captives long to break the boy. When they'd chained up one of the creatures just over a foot away from his face, leaving the child blindfolded, he'd both soiled and wet himself, and his gums had nearly bled from his clamping down so hard on the gag.

And while he had cursed them before, talking to Gabriel, Dylan even prayed to God for his mommy and daddy.

He'd long ago lost track of how long he'd been here, though it'd barely been more than a day. The only way he knew of the nightfall was because of the preacher pleading with God to bring the sun back to show them light.

Dylan had so many questions for the preacher. *Where are we? Who are these people that have us captive? How long have you been here? Are they going to kill me?* But none of them seemed destined to be answered. Not as long as he was gagged, at least.

The door to the barn busted open and Dylan jumped, causing the shackles to pull against his wrists. He cried out through the gag.

"Lord, please protect these children," the preacher said. "Please protect them, and bring forth your sword to strike down these men."

Dylan breathed heavily, the solemn words of the preacher only heightening his nerves. The people loved to come into the barn and toy with him and the other prisoners. They'd, of course, brought the creature in the one time, leaving it there for a time before bashing it with a baseball bat right in front of them. The sound the bat had made, crushing the skull of the beast, was something Dylan would never forget. He only knew it was a bat because one of the men had run the cold aluminum across Dylan's face, leaving trickles of blood to creep down his bare cheek. The cruel laugh that had come from the man's voice said a lot about the people who were holding him captive.

The footsteps now were that of more than one person, and they stopped near where Dylan believed the two girls to be.

"Mmm, which one?" a man asked.

"They're both so pretty," another man said. "Do I really have to choose?"

Dylan heard both the girls crying desperately through their own gags.

"Eeny, meeny, miny, moe," the first man started. Dylan had played this game hundreds of times before, and he pictured the man pointing his finger, alternating back and forth between the two girls.

"Catch a tiger by its toe..."

The two girls whimpered, and Dylan envisioned them with their blindfolds removed. The people had done this to him when they'd stuck the Empty in his face, and he had to think these men would want these two girls to see their faces now as they teased them.

"My mother told me to pick the very best one, and that is... *you*."

One of the girls cried louder now, and the two men laughed.

"Looks like it's your lucky day, baby."

The chains above rattled, and it sounded as if a struggle was going on between the men and at least one of the girls.

"Stop all your fuckin' squirmin'," one of the men demanded, and the chains continued their furious clanking.

There was a loud pop, and that's when the chains calmed.

"Now, I didn't wanna have to go on and hit ya like that, but you gave me no choice. You gonna be good now, or not?"

The room was silent, other than for the shuddered breaths through the gags of the girls and the young boy, and the mumbling of the preacher, as the man waited for a reply from the girl.

"Good," the same man said.

Dylan heard the girl being pulled out of the barn. The other girl, the still restrained one, started to wail again.

The door to the barn creaked and slammed shut. Now the girl next to him tried to scream, the volume muffled by the gag, and the preacher went on.

"Show us the light, Lord. Praise these children, and save them from these evil-doers."

***

When the door opened again, Dylan wasn't certain about how much time had passed. He only knew it had been enough time for him to have fallen asleep, as he'd now been abruptly woken by the double doors' screaming hinges. His blindfold had shifted during his nap, and he was able to see three sets of feet under it. They stopped in front of the preacher, just to the boy's right. Dylan contemplated lifting his head to see their faces, but thought better of it, so as to not draw any attention to himself.

"Ready to try again, preacher?"

For one of the first times since Dylan had ended up here, the preacher spoke words outside of scripture or prayer. He said, "Please, don't make me do this."

The slap echoed through the barn as one of the men hit the preacher.

"You ain't gonna tell us what to do, you got that?"

The preacher whimpered, and started into another prayer. "Oh, Lord, please allow me grace..."

Chains rattled above the preacher's head, and Dylan looked over when he heard the man hit the ground. The preacher had dropped to all fours, grasping the dirt as if, if he held tight enough, the three people wouldn't be able to pick him up off of the ground. But as a man wearing a black t-shirt and a faded baseball cap leaned over to pick him up, the priest made eye contact with Dylan for the first time.

"Bless you, child," the preacher mumbled as the man stood him up straight and dragged him away.

One of the pairs of feet approached Dylan and the boy gasped for air. His blindfold came off, and the last thing he saw before passing out was the back of a bearded man's hand coming down toward his face.

CHAPTER ONE

Gabriel

A short time had passed since David Ellis had thrown Melissa Kessler into the locked room with the Empty. Will and Jessica still remained lying on the ground beside the room, and the rest of the group stood across the hall in utter shock at what had happened. Gabriel had the the sense to start moving people away from the gruesome scene. He left Will alone, allowing him to do what he felt necessary to mourn his mother, but moved the rest of the group down the hallway into a large, vacant room. Jessica had remained behind, as well. Gabriel just wanted to get everyone else away from the scene, but wasn't ready to take everyone back to their living quarters yet. They'd regroup while giving Will and Jessica time to mourn.

Holly had wanted desperately to stay with Will, but Gabriel had encouraged her to give him some time alone. After putting up a small fight, she'd reluctantly agreed, and joined the rest of the group as they trudged away from the murder scene.

After relocating the group down the hall, Gabriel returned to the scene along with Brandon. They moved back around the corner, and saw Will and Jessica in the same spot they'd been. Inside the room, the Empty hissed out of sight.

Brandon walked into a nearby room, and when he came

back, he held a bed sheet under his arm. He walked across the hall and used it to cover Kristen's body. He then approached Gabriel, and reached into his pocket.

"I grabbed this in there, too," Brandon said, revealing a scalpel to Gabriel.

"I got it," Gabriel said, reaching his hand out to retrieve the blade.

Brandon extended his hand, and Gabriel accepted the tool. As he moved toward the door, Gabriel glanced down at Will. He didn't even acknowledge Gabriel's presence, simply staring off at the opposite wall. Gabriel looked up and reached for the door, and pulled it.

Opening the door was like turning up the volume on the inside of the room. The creature growled and moaned as it continued to feast on its kill. Gabriel put aside the thought that it was Will's mother lying on the ground, and he carefully moved toward the beast. Just as he came just within reach of it, the Empty turned and hissed at him. Gabriel reacted quickly, bringing the scalpel into the side of the creature's head. It slumped over, and Gabriel turned away right as Mrs. Kessler came into view, but not before he caught a glance of what remained of her corpse. He leaned over and coughed, then hurried out of the room.

Brandon shut the door behind Gabriel, who retched, just holding back from vomiting all over the floor. Brandon patted him on the shoulder.

"You alright?" Brandon asked.

Gabriel looked up. "Yeah, yeah. I'm fine." He wiped at his mouth, cleaning the saliva from his lips. "Come on, let's move Marcus."

Brandon went back into the same room where he'd found a scalpel and returned this time with a mobile bed. They each lifted an end of Marcus' limp body, and loaded the unconscious man onto the bed. Brandon began to push Marcus down the hall, while Gabriel gave Will one last glance. He still sat in the same spot, Jessica crying next to him, his face vacant of any emotion.

Gabriel understood the fight ahead. Will would want to seek revenge, there was no doubt of that. And Gabriel would back the decision, but he also knew they would need a plan. He wouldn't allow Will to just march out of the hospital like a loose canon. He was confident that, wherever David was headed, Dylan would be there. In Gabriel's mind, the boy's safety was the number one priority now. There was nothing they could do about Mrs. Kessler. She was gone. But they had to find Dylan and bring him back into the group safely. Gabriel was responsible for the boy being taken, and he was determined to be the one responsible for getting him back. The boy dying wasn't an option. Gabriel would put a bullet in his own head before he'd live every day of the rest of his life with *that* guilt.

When Marcus finally came to, Holly was the one who decided to explain to him everything that had happened. When she was finished, he joined Gabriel in the hallway while the rest of the group stayed in the large room.

"How you feeling?" Gabriel asked.

"Like shit. I feel like I got hit with two ton of bricks."

"Sorry about that, man."

"Why you sorry?" Marcus asked. "Don't worry about me." Marcus nodded his head down the hall toward the place they'd come from. The place where Melissa's body still lay. "What we gonna do about Will?"

"I don't know," Gabriel replied. "But I'm gonna need your help with keeping him from doing anything stupid. He's gonna be emotional, ready to go raise hell on David. You know as well as I do, we can't just rush in there without a plan."

Marcus scoffed. "That shouldn't be a problem. We don't even know where *there* is."

Gabriel was silent, and he let his head rest against the wall as he shut his eyes.

When he opened his eyes and looked over to Marcus, he noted, "It's my fault he's gone, Marcus. I was careless. I should have never let him out of my sight."

"Come on, man. You had no way of knowing that asshole was gonna find us. Hell, I thought he was dead."

"He should've been," Gabriel said, regret in his voice. "We shouldn't have left that warehouse with him still breathing."

"And had we done that, what would that have really said about us? What kind of person do you want to be?"

"The kind who doesn't let children get kidnapped and people's mothers get eaten alive by those fucking things."

"At the time, killing David wasn't the answer. You know that."

"Yeah?" Gabriel continued. "Well, what about now?"

Marcus looked to the ground and rubbed his eyes. Shaking his head, he then moved his hands to his hips.

Exhaling, Marcus looked up to Gabriel and said, "I think we both know what needs to be done."

***

Will

He simply sat there. No movement. No talking. Just still and silent.

Will's back lay against the wall underneath the window. He had one knee up with his arm resting on top, his foot flat on the ground. Just on the other side of the wall lay his mother and the beast that had killed her. Though, the real beast that had killed her had escaped.

Will stared into the wall opposite him, and all he saw in it was the face of David Ellis.

Just a week earlier, Will had been a forklift operator at one of the world's most popular cymbal and percussion manufacturers. When the world fell, he'd looked on as all his co-workers had been destroyed. He now lived in a world full of flesh-eating creatures, and those things weren't even his biggest threat or enemy. This man, who owned a company just down the road from where he'd worked for so long, had taken his own mother from him. And for what? Will had no answer.

Will thought back to when they'd left Ellis Metals. David had just been lying there on the ground, unconscious. Why had he let him live? If he would have just killed the man right there, none of this would be happening. He'd have his mother, and they'd be thriving at the hospital, working through the trouble of this new world together.

But it wasn't to be.

Then there was Jessica—the girl who had apparently come to love his mother. She'd been lying next to him, but had moved some time ago. She now sat across the hall, weeping. After having sat in the same spot for some time, turning over all his emotions in his mind, Will decided to go to her.

He stood up and breathed heavily, ignoring the urge to turn around and look inside the room. He closed his eyes and walked over to the corner where Jessica sat.

When he approached her, she looked up from her arms where she'd buried her head. Her eyes were beet-red and she looked exhausted. Will took a seat next to her, and she immediately leaned into his arms and started to cry again.

"I'm so sorry," she said.

Will remained silent. He still couldn't find the words to speak. His face stoic, he just held her and comforted her with his presence while his mind wandered.

But Will couldn't just sit anymore. He looked over toward the room, knowing his mother was lying in there. He had to get away.

And with that, Will stood and headed down the hallway.

***

Gabriel

"How much longer are we just going to let them sit down there?" Holly asked.

"As long as he needs to," Marcus replied.

"We can't do that," Holly explained. "What if he does something to himself? He just lost his mother!"

"Holly—"

"I'm going down there," she said, and started out of the room. Brandon grabbed onto her shoulder.

"Marcus is right," Brandon said. "You need to just give him some time. He will snap out of it, then we can all come up with a plan together."

10

"Get your hands off me," Holly demanded.

"Come on, Holly," Marcus said, trying to calm her down.

Gabriel stood near the door, away from the crowd. He leaned his back against the wall, watching as the group argued amongst themselves. His head pounded, overwhelmed by the thought that Dylan was out there somewhere, the boy likely terrified and waiting on them to come and get him. He was just about to raise his own voice and shut the group up when he heard footsteps coming down the hall.

It caught the rest of the group's attention, and they stood quiet.

Gabriel watched as Will moved past the room, and when he turned to look at the group, Marcus was already headed after their friend. Holly tried to follow, but Gabriel stopped her.

"Just wait here," he demanded.

"No, I'm not—"

"Just do it, Holly!" He was demanding, but he knew that he and Marcus needed to handle it. He then calmed his tone. "Please, just stay here with the others. Marcus and I got this."

He turned and started after Marcus and Will.

***

Gabriel followed them all the way to the main corridor where the survivors had been living. When he raced through the double doors near the elevators and moved around the corner, his eyes went wide.

Will and Marcus were each fighting off an Empty. Will had his assailant pinned against a wall, while Marcus struggled to stay on his feet in the middle of the hall. The thing had its hands around Marcus' neck as the other man made eye contact with Gabriel.

"Help! Get this thing off me!"

Their firearms having been stolen by David, Gabriel scanned the room for a weapon, finally deciding to pull a fire extinguisher off of the wall. He darted over to Marcus and reached him just as the thing pushed him down onto the ground. The creature looked up toward Gabriel, who swung the fire extinguisher as hard as he could, leveling the beast in the face. Gabriel spun around, dropping the weapon as he did. He then stepped up beside the Empty, which reached for him, and slammed his foot down onto the creature's face, looking away so he couldn't see the result; the grotesque sound and the feeling underfoot provided plenty of sensory confirmation.

He then turned and saw Marcus scooting on the ground toward a wall, staring over toward Will.

Will was on top of the beast he'd been fighting, the fire extinguisher in hand. He wouldn't stop continuing the assault, bringing the metal down into the Empty's face again and again. Blood sprayed up from either side of Will's body, and he'd begun to yell.

Gabriel took his eyes off of Will and looked down the hall. The rest of the group was starting to gather, Holly at the front. She had a look of shock and terror on her face, covering half of it with her hands as tears poured out of each eye. The rest of the group shared similar looks. All except for Jessica, who stood with her hands at her sides, just watching the assault on the creature.

Will continued, and Gabriel didn't think he was even aware that everyone was looking on.

Marcus went to Will, and Gabriel followed. Together, they pulled Will off of the Empty. He nearly hit Gabriel in the face with the fire extinguisher, and Gabriel managed to wrangle it from his hands.

"Easy, easy," Gabriel said.

"Come on, Will. Ease up, kid," Marcus added.

Gabriel was taken back by the look in Will's eyes. He looked like a man possessed. Blood now covered his face and he gasped for air. His eyes were wide, and he stared down into the creature's face.

"Will, come on, snap out of it," Gabriel said.

Will looked over to Gabriel, those eyes still spread, but his breathing starting to level off. After a few moments, he was breathing almost normally, and his eyes relaxed.

Then he let go.

Will hugged Gabriel, allowing all his emotion to come out. He cried in his friend's arms. Gabriel held him close, running his hand up and down Will's back.

Holly ran to them, and she wrapped her arms around the two of them, letting her own tears go.

Gabriel held them both, as if they were his younger siblings, while the rest of the group watched. He thought again of Dylan, and hoped that he'd have the chance to hug the boy soon.

CHAPTER TWO

Jessica

After Holly had taken Will into his room and the rest of the group had settled, Jessica stole a moment to speak with Gabriel and Marcus. She invited them into her room and asked them to sit.

"What's up?" Marcus asked.

"I know why those two things were out there," Jessica started. "Will left me in a closet after those men arrived. I was actually just about to come and look for you all when I heard David and those other two guys come running down the hallway."

"What the hell happened to them?" Gabriel asked.

"David shot them."

"Son of a bitch," Marcus said, sitting back in his chair. "Dude has gone totally off his rocker."

"Well, he did shoot that nurse right in front of us and then throw a woman into a cage to be slaughtered by one of those things," Gabriel added, then noticing the change in Jessica's face when he brought up Melissa's death. "Sorry."

"It's okay," she said, wiping at her eyes. "He was on the radio with someone when he killed them. He was lying, saying that you guys were the ones that shot them."

"Shit," Gabriel said. "He's trying to pin this on us so they'll come after us."

"Why would he do that?" Jessica asked. "Why didn't he just kill you all while he was here?"

"Because that's too easy," Marcus said. "We left him for dead in a warehouse. He doesn't want us to go easy—especially Will."

After a few moments of silence, Jessica continued. "The man on the other end of the radio gave David directions to where they are."

This caught Gabriel's attention. "You know where he went?"

Jessica nodded.

"And you remember the directions?" Marcus asked.

"We take I-40 West to the Waverly Road exit. We head down the road a couple of miles and we should find the place. It's a farm. I think they said it was called Hopkins Farm."

"It's gotta be the same place Dylan is," Gabriel said. He looked over to Marcus. "We've gotta go there."

Marcus put his arms out with his palms up. "With what? A bunch of syringes and scalpels?"

"So, what? We just stay here and wait for them to come and slaughter us?"

"I didn't say that," Marcus said. "But you said yourself, we've gotta be level-headed and have a plan before we just march out of here and go all Rambo on them."

"Maybe we should take all this to the rest of the group," Jessica suggested. "Some of them are from the area, right? So, maybe one of them will have an idea of somewhere we can find some weapons."

"Good idea," Marcus said.

"We've gotta make sure we have a plan that's not just going in there guns blazing. If we do that, they might hurt the kid," Jessica said.

Jessica saw that Gabriel was clearly uncomfortable talking about the boy, and just as he looked like he might get upset, Marcus put his hand on Gabriel's shoulder.

"Agreed," Marcus said. "Nothing is gonna happen to Dylan."

***

Will

It was the first time that Will and Holly had been able to be alone together since they'd met. And even though Holly was there with him, Will felt the most alone he ever had in his entire life.

They lay in bed cuddled up next to each other. Holly's head was nestled into Will's bare chest, which she'd wet with tears. He lay on his back, staring at the ceiling and running his hand through her hair. The room still held the slightly humid air of the shower. When they'd first come into the room after Will had pummeled the Empty in the hallway, until its face had looked like tenderized meat, Holly had immediately stripped him down so he could take a shower. Later on, he'd probably be disappointed that this was the first time she'd seen him naked. She had thrown his clothes into a bag and then tossed it into the hallway, and that was the only time they'd opened the door since coming inside the room. He'd allowed her to stay in the bathroom with him while he'd showered, sensing that she was worried he may try to hurt himself if left alone. But he had no interest in hurting himself—only in killing David Ellis. And as he lay on the bed now, facing the ceiling, he continued to see David's face everywhere he looked. It was as if it were painted as a mural across the popcorn texture above him.

Holly's embrace did bring *some* comfort to him. She obviously didn't want him to be in pain, and it hurt her to see him like this.

"Everything's gonna be okay," she said, breaking their extended mutual silence.

"Not until I kill him."

She shifted onto her elbow, but continued to rub his chest and his stomach.

"I know you're hurting inside. I do. But how are you so sure that killing him is going to make you feel any better?"

The question was enough to finally draw his attention away from the ceiling to look down to her.

"Do you want me to just let him stay out there and get off scot-free?"

"I'm not saying that, but—"

"But what, Holly? That piece of shit fed my mother to a goddamn monster right in front of me. Do you realize what I saw? I'll never get that image out of my head. And until I kill that son of a bitch, I'm gonna see his smirking grin everywhere I look."

Holly moved from her elbow to her back and started to cry again.

"I'm sorry, Holly," Will said, lowering his voice. "I just don't understand how you expect me to forget about him and not want to go after him."

"I know you're frustrated and angry, I just don't want you to get hurt," she said through a series of sniffs and gasps as she tried to stop crying.

Will rolled over toward her and wiped the tears away from her cheeks. Then he leaned down and kissed her on the lips, running his hands through her hair.

"I'm not going to get hurt. Neither are you, or Marcus, or anybody here."

She rubbed the stubble on his face and then leaned up far enough to kiss his mouth, running her fingertips on her other hand down his stomach.

A familiar feeling returned to Will. One that he hadn't even thought about since before he'd woken up in that tiny office at Element just days ago as the world had been turning to shit. Now, of all times, the slight burn came to him, and he couldn't think of a better way to rid his tensions in this moment.

He rolled over onto Holly and pulled the covers on top of them.

***

About an hour later, Will stepped out of the room.

Sarah, one of the nurses who worked at the hospital, was sitting in a chair just across the hall and looked up when he came out of the room.

"Hi," she said.

"Hey."

"Gabriel asked if someone could hang outside of your room."

"In case I ran away?"

She blushed. "To let them know when you came out."

"Right," he said, cracking a little smile. "I can go let them know myself. Where are they?"

She pointed down the hall to his left. "Just down there and through that open door. There's a break room back there, and everyone should be waiting."

"You want to walk with me down there and join us?" Will offered.

Sarah shook her head. "I've seen a lot of messed up stuff today, even for a nurse. I think I just need to lie down for a little while."

"I understand." He smiled at her and then started toward the break room.

"I'm really sorry about your mother," Sarah mumbled.

Will stopped and stood still for a moment before he turned around. "Thank you." He nodded and then continued, down the hall and through the open door.

CHAPTER THREE

<u>Jessica</u>

It had been a while since Jessica had eaten anything, and she finally felt hungry again. Everyone else in the hospital seemed to be just waiting on Will to come out of his room, and she had retreated to her own space to rest for a while. Now, she walked out of her room into an empty corridor and headed for the break room.

When she walked into the break room, she was surprised to see everyone sitting inside, Will included.

"Oh, hey," she said. "Sorry."

She started to turn around until a voice stopped her.

"Where're you going?"

Jessica turned around and saw that Gabriel was the one who'd asked the question.

"I was hoping you'd stay," he told her. "You're part of this group now, so your input is important to the decisions we make."

"Oh," Jessica said. "Okay."

She was still shy around the group. One would have thought that a hotel's front desk clerk would have no problem being social and bonding with new people, but that wasn't the case with Jessica. She was an introvert, and like most introverts, she gained energy when she was alone as opposed to being around other people. The job at the hotel had been just that: a job. The same way introverted lead singers of rock bands could jump on stage without missing a lyric or throwing up from nervousness, Jessica had been able to act her way through her job on most days.

There was an open seat next to Will, and she took it.

"We're discussing what our next move is gonna be," Marcus informed her.

She felt a tap on her arm and looked over to Will.

"They told me that you know where David went. That you overheard directions on his radio. That true?"

Jessica nodded.

"And he really killed those other two guys?" Sam asked.

Again, Jessica nodded. "I didn't see it, but I heard the gunshots."

"The guy must have no soul," Brandon added.

"He doesn't," Will said sternly.

"So," Jessica began, "what are you guys thinking about doing?"

Gabriel pointed his thumb toward Brandon. "Brandon's parents live only a thirty minute drive from here."

"And that's in five o'clock traffic. Not sure we'll be hitting that," Brandon said, smirking.

"So, we're gonna go stay there?" Jessica asked.

Brandon shook his head. "My old man has a small arsenal there. He's real into his guns. Almost obsessively."

"If he lives so close to here, why isn't he here with us?" Jessica asked. "I'd have figured you guys would've hooked up by now."

Holly came into the room, and Jessica saw her smile at Will. He offered her his chair since there wasn't an open one, but she declined, telling him she'd rather stand.

"He's down in Florida spending time with some woman who's probably gonna become my step-mom. Well, I assume she still might be. Given how everything has gone to shit, who knows?"

"We just gotta hope the neighbors or someone else hasn't already raided his stash," Marcus said.

"We're gonna go there; then we're gonna go to that farm," Will added.

"Well, not *right* to the farm," Gabriel corrected, "but that's the plan. We've got to be well-equipped so we can get Dylan back here safely."

"Who all's going to that house?" Jessica asked.

"Just Will and I," Brandon told her.

"Just the two of you?" Jessica asked. "That's crazy. How much time have you guys spent out there? Do you know how nuts it is?"

Holly, who'd been quiet up until now, scowled at Jessica. "Do we know how nuts it is? We've spent plenty of goddamn time out there. You think we've just been sittin' in here on our thumbs?"

"That's not what—"

"We had to scratch and claw our way here," Holly continued. She pointed at Jessica as she spoke, her tone turning increasingly dark. "We lost people out there and we had a shit ton of other close calls. So, yeah, I think you could say we know how 'nuts' it is out there."

"Holly, calm down," Will said. "This isn't helping the situation. Jessica hasn't had a chance to really get to know us yet and hear our stories."

22

"No shit," Holly added.

"Seriously, Holly. Will is right—you're not helping us get any closer to finding Dylan," Marcus added.

"So now you want to gang up on me?" Holly said. She turned around and stormed out of the room.

Will called after her, but she disappeared.

"Just let her go," Marcus said. "I've known that girl a long time, she'll be fine."

"I'm sorry," Jessica mumbled. "I wasn't trying to offend anyone."

"It's okay. She just doesn't want me going out there right now," Will said.

"You can't go with just the two of you," Jessica reiterated.

"I'll go," Sam said.

Will nodded. "I want Gabriel and Marcus to stay behind and help look after the hospital. Just in case anyone shows up here who could be a threat."

"I understand," Jessica said. "But I still want to go with you."

"Why would you want to do that?" Gabriel asked.

"I want to contribute to your group. I'm the newest one here, and I want to pull my weight."

"You can contribute here at the hospital," Marcus said.

"Oh yeah, how? Want me to do some laundry? Cook some food? Or sit out in the hallway like that nurse did to make sure no one tries to run away to off themselves?"

Immediately, she regretted that last line and she looked over to Will. "I'm sorry."

"No, it's okay." He looked over to Gabriel and Marcus. "We'll take her with us."

Gabriel looked surprised. "You sure that's a good idea?"

Will nodded. "She helped get my mother here, and my father saw something in her enough to risk his own life for her. If she wants to go with us, I think she should be able to make that decision herself." He looked over to her and smiled. "Clearly, she can hold her own."

Jessica returned the smile. "Thank you."

Marcus clapped his hands together one time and looked to Will. "Alright, so when y'all headed out?"

Before he could answer, Sarah came rushing into the room.

"I need to show you guys something," Sarah said. "Please, come quick, it's important."

***

Gabriel

The group stood on the bridge that separated the main corridor from the parking garage. To either side of them, the large windows showed that the sun had almost disappeared for the night, but there was still just enough light to see about a half dozen Empties lumbering along on the road below.

Everyone looked on in silence.

Pummeling sounded from the door in front of them; it was the exit that led out into the parking garage. And through the small window in the solid metal frame, a group of Empties fought to have their faces seen.

"I was just going to go out to get some fresh air, and I heard the banging as soon as I walked onto the bridge," Sarah explained.

Gabriel walked to the door as the rest of the group

24

remained silent behind him. The window was filled with faces. The most prominent had been a male—the bushy beard, once gray but now stained with human blood, still prominent on its face. Though the creatures filled the space of the small window, they kept pushing each other out of the way enough for him to be able to see past them in quick glimpses. Not only was the makeshift gate the group had built open, but it had been crashed through. Gabriel could see shards of the boards scattered over the concrete.

"Looks like David didn't bother to close the gate behind him," Will said. "Don't think we'll be repairing it anytime soon."

"Shit," Marcus grumbled. "How in the hell are we supposed to get them out of here now?"

The Empties seemed to be banging and growling louder now that they could see human flesh, and that combined with the commotion of a few members of the group prevented Gabriel from thinking properly. He put his hands behind his head and bowed it, crushing his eyes shut.

"Everyone, shut up!"

Gabriel looked up and noticed Will's scowl. He was also looking toward Gabriel, clearly seeing that they were equally frustrated.

"Let's take this shit inside where we can actually think straight without these things about to punch that damn door down, and we'll come up with a plan," Will said. He turned around and headed back inside, the rest of the group following.

Gabriel took one last look back toward the door, staring into the starving faces of the undead. Outside, the sky had only minutes of daylight left. Below, the street was empty, and Gabriel wondered if the beasts who had been there were now headed upstairs to join their friends.

***

When Gabriel walked back inside the hospital, the rest of the group had already gathered near the nurses' station to discuss what their next action should be.

"The staircase over there is the one we hauled the bodies into," Brandon said, pointing to a door just a few doors down from the break room. "We put them all the way down at the bottom and blocked the door, so even if we wanted to try getting past all the dead bodies without getting sick to our stomachs, that door is still blocked. And I don't think anyone is touching those things."

"So, our only option is to use the staircase down by the elevators then, right?" Will asked. He was thinking of the story he'd been told earlier about how one of the survivors at the hospital had been killed the last time they'd tried to go downstairs.

Brandon nodded. "That's the closest to the garage, no doubt." He pointed down the long hallway toward the elevators. "We're still gonna have a nice little run for it to the garage. Luckily, the general layout of the floor is about the same, so we should have a basic idea about how far we'll have to go."

"What're you going to do about a car once you get out there?" Holly asked.

Brandon gave Will a puzzled look and said, "Maybe we could still get to the ambulance once we get out there."

Marcus scoffed. "There could be fifty of those things

waiting to get in here to us and surrounding that ambulance. Gonna have to come up with a better plan than that."

Gabriel finally spoke up. "Do any of you know how to hotwire a car?"

"Pretty much," Will said.

Gabriel tilted his head and narrowed his eyes at Will. "Pretty much?"

"I sure as hell don't know how," Sam said.

"Maybe you should just let me go," Gabriel said. "I had to—"

"No," Will said, cutting him off. "I can handle it."

"Should we even be doing this at night?" Sam asked.

"It'll be fine," Will replied.

"That's a good point," Jessica added. "We should wait until morning. It won't be as dangerous."

"We aren't waiting 'til morning," Will told her. "We're going tonight. For all we know, those hicks could be on their way here now, and it'd be just like pickin' fish out of a barrel if they showed up. We'd all be dead in minutes."

Gabriel could see the frustration mounting on Will's face. He looked over to Marcus, curious if he'd speak up and protest. Marcus just gave a slight shrug. Gabriel sensed a fine line in how to approach Will. Even though he was acting more like himself now, this was still a man who'd lost his mother just hours earlier, and learned about the death of his father not too long before that.

"We'll be alright," Brandon assured them. "I've seen someone hotwire a car before, so I think between the two of us that we'll figure it out."

Gabriel sighed. "Okay." He looked over to Jessica and

asked, "You cool with this?"

She looked slightly hesitant, but nodded.

"Guess we better try and find something you can use to at least shoo them away with if any Empties come after you," Marcus said, trying to lighten the mood. It got a laugh out of a couple of people, including Will, but Gabriel remained stoic.

All he wanted was for the group to get to those guns, and move one step closer to reaching Dylan.

CHAPTER FOUR

Jessica

Sitting on the edge of her bed, Jessica tried on the tennis shoes that Sarah had brought her. They'd belonged to Kristen, the nurse who David had killed.

They were only about a half size too large, which was perfectly fine with Jessica. She knew she'd be able to maneuver in them much more easily than in her work shoes, which would be important when they left for Brandon's father's house.

Once the laces were tied on both shoes, she stood up to test the comfort of them. She jogged in place for a few moments before walking over to the large window at the other end of the room. The shoes were comfortable, and her ankle felt good from her earlier injury. She'd opened the curtains earlier in the day in hopes of improving her mood with sunshine. Now, the moon gently lit the room. The stars were out, and she gave herself a moment to admire them. She looked down and could see one of the creatures moving across the sidewalk, under a lamp post. The two lights on either side of it had reached the end of their kindling, leaving an extended stretch of darkness over the pavement.

Jessica was nervous about going on this run.

Not only would getting to a vehicle be a challenge, but then they had to get it started. Then, even if those two things happened, they'd be traveling for half an hour in the dead of night to a place that she was unfamiliar with. Despite the danger, though, Jessica did agree with Will. The risk was well worth it. If the people from the farm showed up to avenge their deceased, everyone in the group would be dead.

A knock came at the door and she turned back. It was Holly.

"They're just about ready," she said.

"Oh, thank you."

Holly stepped all the way into the room and shut the door behind her.

"I'm really sorry about earlier," Holly said. "I didn't mean to offend you."

"It's okay. You didn't offend me," Jessica said. "I'm sorry for what I said about you guys not knowing what it's like out there."

Holly nodded. "It's just been a really tough day, you know? And I'm just really scared about Will going out there. I'm really worried he's just going to be careless."

"If you're scared he's going to do something irrational to get himself killed tonight, I'd quit worrying so much about it," Jessica told her. "From what I see, he's not even gonna sleep until he gets his hands on David."

Holly took her hands up either side of her head and moved her hair back behind her ears.

"Just promise me you'll keep a close eye on him," Holly said.

Nodding and moving her bangs to the side, Jessica agreed. "I promise I'll keep an eye on him."

"Thanks," Holly mumbled. "I really appreciate it. And

when you get back, maybe we can sit down and have a cup of coffee together or something."

"I'd like that," Jessica replied, smiling.

There was another knock on the door, and when it opened, Marcus appeared.

"Hey, you comin'? They're waiting on you."

Jessica looked down at her feet, wiggling her toes and bouncing her heels a few times to continue adjusting to the broken-in shoes.

"Yeah, I'll be right there."

Marcus nodded and then looked to Holly. "Will wants to see you before he leaves."

"Alright," Holly said.

Marcus headed back down the hallway and Holly gave Jessica another smile before she turned and walked out the door.

***

Will

Will sat at the edge of his bed with his hands clasped together, staring down at the floor. His mind had been overtaken by thoughts of his dead parents and of David Ellis. In truth, he knew he wasn't focused enough to go out on this gun run. But he didn't care. Sitting around in the hospital only meant he would continue to think about his mother's description of how his father had turned into an Empty, then come after her. And then he would replay that scene in his mind—of David throwing his helpless mother into that room with the beast and making him watch the fallout. Will needed a purpose to give his mind a break, and this gun run would be the perfect outlet.

A gentle knock came at the door and he looked up to see Holly entering. The overhead lights were off, the lamps above the bed giving the room its only illumination. Even through the shadows, Will could see the concern spread across Holly's face. She stopped halfway between the bed and the door with her arms crossed. Will sat up and let his arms rest on his thighs.

Holly bowed her head to the floor and mumbled, "I don't want you to go."

"I know."

"Then why are you doing this?" She looked up at him now. "Just let Gabriel or Marcus go."

"I can't."

Holly scoffed. "Great, now I'm just getting two word answers out of you."

Silence filled the room while Will collected himself. He was facing the ground again with his eyes closed when he said, "I'm too dangerous to stay here right now."

"What do you mean?"

He looked up at her again. "I mean that, if I stay here, I could end up hurting someone."

Her eyes went wide and she looked as if she wanted to cry.

"I feel like a caged animal in here right now. I can't just sit in this place and do nothing. I'll go mad."

She moved beside him and rubbed his shoulder with her hand.

"We don't have to sit around and do nothing, sweetie. I can cook us some supper. I make a mean microwave dinner." This got a slight laugh out of Will, and Holly moved her hand up to the back of his neck. "Then I can do plenty of things to distract your mind." She ran her hand around the side of his neck, rubbing it.

"That isn't good enough," Will replied.

The next few moments went by in a blur. Those four words had just poured out before Will could realize what he was saying—the grip on his neck loosened and Holly stepped away from him

"What did you say?" Holly asked.

Will looked up at her and she was glaring at him.

"Holly, that's not what I meant."

"Well, what exactly did you mean? 'Cause that sure as hell sounded like you don't give two shits about what happened earlier."

Will sighed. "Come on, Holly. All I'm saying is that I got caught in the moment. Needless to say, the timing kinda sucked."

"Are you saying you 'anger-fucked' me?"

Will stood and rolled his eyes. "I don't have time for this petty bullshit."

Holly's eyes filled with tears as she started to back away from him. What was strange to Will was that he didn't feel guilty about any of it, and he was sure the look on his face showed that. She shook her head, then turned and stormed out of the room.

When she was gone, Will drew in deep, heavy breaths. He walked over to the wall and braced himself against it with both his hands. Dark energy rose inside him and he could feel the blood rush. When he looked up, he realized he'd come to a place at the wall where a mirror was just in front of him. He saw the blood and the paleness in his eyes. A version of himself he'd never seen before stared back at him. One filled with anger and hate. In an instant, he reared back his fist and punched the mirror as hard as he could, causing the whole mirror to crack, growing out like a spiderweb.

Blood pooled on the floor as Will clinched his fists, looking back at his worn face through the broken mirror.

***

Jessica

The rest of the group stood in the hallway, waiting on Will. Moments earlier, they'd seen Holly exit the room in tears. Marcus had followed her down the hall, and neither of them had come back. Jessica looked over to Brandon, seeing that he appeared even more nervous than she did. She knew he'd been on plenty of runs before, and wondered why he was so nervous about this one.

"You sure you want to do this?"

Jessica looked over and saw Gabriel standing next to her. She nodded her head.

"What about your shoulder?" he asked.

"It feels fine, really. You guys aren't going to stop me from going."

Gabriel smiled. "Fair enough."

The door to Will's room opened, garnering everyone's attention. Jessica's eyes immediately went to his hand. It was wrapped in what had once been a white towel, which he clutched with his opposite hand. Most of the white color of the towel was gone, replaced by stains of his blood.

Brandon looked over to Sarah as he walked toward Will. "Go grab something to clean and wrap it in, quick. Let me see that."

"It's fine," Will said. "No big deal." Will pulled the towel away and revealed a laceration across the middle knuckle on his left hand.

"Shit, man," Brandon said. He leaned in to observe the wound. "You're gonna need stitches."

"What the hell did you do?" Gabriel asked him.

Will shook his head. "Don't worry about it. I'm fine." He then looked back over to Brandon. "How long will it take to stitch me up?"

"Shouldn't take but a few minutes, but I can't do it. I don't know how."

Sarah came back with some gauze and a bottle of peroxide to disinfect the wound.

"Can you do stitches?" Brandon asked Sarah.

She shook her head. "I've never done it, but I could try."

"I'll do it."

They looked over at Jessica.

"You've done this before?" Sarah asked.

"Well, not on a human. Or with skin. But I've sewn since I was nine years old."

Brandon and Sarah looked at each other, and Brandon shrugged.

"Alright. I'll go grab the supplies you'll need and Sarah can set you up with a spot to do it."

***

Sarah prepared one of the small observation rooms for Jessica to stitch up Will's hand. While grabbing the supplies, Brandon retrieved a light numbing agent and administered the shot into Will's hand so he wouldn't feel the needle.

When they had finished getting the room ready, Brandon and Sarah left Jessica alone with Will to stitch up his hand.

She ran the needle through his skin as he faced the wall and refused to watch. Once the bleeding had mostly ceased and she could see the wound, it was a fairly easy task. She treated it just like one of her craft projects, and it made her miss the hours she'd spent putting little pieces of art together.

"Thanks for doing this," Will said, still looking toward the wall.

"It's no problem. I don't even think those other two wanted to try."

Will chuckled. "Yeah, I was getting a little worried myself. Honestly, I'm surprised you're able to do this with your arm hurting."

"Well, if I'm being honest with you, I think Lawrence didn't really know what he was talking about. I'm pretty sure I just have a minor sprain or something, not a broken collarbone. A lot of my movement has come back—I just still have some discomfort."

"Gotcha," Will replied.

"Dare I ask how this happened?" Jessica asked.

Like the rest of the group, she'd seen Holly leave the room abruptly, and though she wasn't the type to gossip, Jessica still found herself a little curious.

"Just not a good day," he replied.

"Yeah. You could say that."

After a few moments of awkward silence, Will spoke again.

"Sounds like you really got pretty close to my folks over a

short period of time."

"I was inches away from being eaten by one of those things when your dad opened their door and pulled me into their room. Then he kept them off your mother and I so we could get away, and got bit himself in the process. I owe everything to that man." She pulled away from his hand for a moment to gather herself. She wasn't crying, but she was fighting back tears. Then, she leaned in and continued. "And your mom was there for me when we found my parents. I was ready to lay down and die beside them, but she wouldn't let me. She made me get up and keep going."

Will was quiet after that, and just continued to stare at the wall.

"All she wanted was to find you," Jessica continued. "That was one of the things that kept me going. I felt I owed her that."

For the first time since she had started sewing up his hand, Will looked away from the wall and peered into Jessica's eyes. She had a couple of tears running down her cheek, and he used his free hand to reach over and wipe them off one side of her face with his thumb.

"Thank you for helping her find me," he said softly.

Her only response was to smile at him. Then she wiped her eyes as he pulled his un-injured hand away and allowed her to continue working on the stitches.

A few minutes later, she set the needle down on a nearby table.

"All done," Jessica said.

Will looked down at his hand. "Thanks."

"No problem. Now let's get ready to get out of here."

CHAPTER FIVE

Will

The group gathered at the end of the long hallway by the elevators. Opposite the elevators were two doorways. One of them led to the staircase that would take Will, Brandon, Jessica, and Sam to the level below, and the other housed the double doors that went back to the wing where David had taken the group earlier in the day.

They stood in front of the stairway entrance, but Will found himself staring at the double doors.

Deep down, he wanted to rush through the doors and sprint back to the area where his mother had been killed. Her body was still back there. Part of the reason Will wanted to go with the others was because he knew Gabriel was going to lead a clean-up of that room while he was gone, and pull his mother out in the process. He wanted to be away when that happened, and he could guess that this was also part of the reason Gabriel had shown little resistance to him going.

Will turned away from the door when he felt a hand grip his shoulder.

"You about ready?" Gabriel asked.

Will nodded. He looked down at the broomstick he held in his hands and chuckled. "Ready as I'll ever be."

The best thing they'd been able to find for weapons were some mops and brooms in a supply closet. They'd taken the heads off of them to create three makeshift Bo Staffs. They'd also found kitchen knives in the break room, and the four of them each carried one of those on them as well, but the broom sticks would give them a little more range. They'd agreed that the best strategy was going to be to run like hell down the hallway and reach the garage as quickly as possible. There was no need to take out the Empties—only to get past them. But, in truth, they had no idea how many of the creatures would be down there.

Will looked over to Brandon, who had sweat dripping down his cheeks. He nervously rotated his staff in his hands with sweaty palms. Standing next to Brandon, Sam looked much the same. His eyes were closed and his lips moved as he mumbled something to himself.

Then he looked over to Jessica. Her arm was out of the sling and she was moving it around, trying to loosen it up. Apparently, she'd been right about the misdiagnosis the EMT had given her. It didn't look like her arm would be a hindrance. Aside for this first part of their journey, her legs were going to be much more important anyway.

"You ready?" Will asked her.

"Yeah," Jessica replied. She had a focused look in her eyes.

He felt a presence from his other side and looked over to see Holly. She rubbed her eyes with her free hand, and her other arm was crossed over her chest. Her face was flush, and she looked exhausted.

"I still don't want you to go," she mumbled.

"I know," Will said.

"But I know you have to." There was a pause as they

39

stared at each other, and then she said, "I'm sorry about earlier." She looked down at his wrapped hand, the gauze having a light stain of blood to it.

"Don't be," Will told her. "I was an asshole. You've done nothing but tried to be supportive today."

The last line made her smile, and she leaned in to hug him.

As she cried on his shoulder, Will's eyes wandered to Jessica, who was looking at them with that same serious and focused look on her face. She cracked a small smile, then turned away, moving her hair out of her face. Will pulled away from Holly.

"Just get back to me safe, okay?" Holly said.

Will leaned in and kissed her on the forehead, then embraced her. "I will. I promise."

She stepped away from him, holding his hand until she had backed up to join the rest of the group, standing next to Marcus as he clutched her from the side. Gabriel then approached Will again. He reached his hand out and Will took it.

"Everything will be handled when you get back," Gabriel told him.

Will pulled him into a fast hug. "Thanks, bro. I really appreciate it."

They pulled apart and Gabriel said, "No problem. Now go get us some guns so we can go get that son of a bitch and rescue Dylan."

Will nodded, then turned toward the stairway door. He, Sam, Brandon, and Jessica stood in a line facing it. He opened the door, and they headed inside.

They reached the bottom of the first ten steps, then turned around the corner for a slightly longer descent.

When they reached the bottom, Will put his ear to the door. There wasn't a window pane, so the only way to know if there was something waiting for them on the other side of the metal frame would be to listen. He looked over to his cohorts and shook his head.

Above them, the group looked down to them from the top of the wrapped staircase. Will looked up to give Gabriel and Marcus a thumbs up, and then winked at Holly. The group above retreated back through the door.

He glanced over his shoulder.

"Ready?" he whispered.

The three people with him nodded.

"Alright, watch my back."

Will closed his eyes and drew in a deep breath. His hand grasped the metal handle and he opened the door.

***

Light on the 7th floor of the hospital appeared to be almost non-existent. In spots, the overhead lamps flickered, illuminating some of the shadows. There was a strong buzzing sound that came from the bulbs, and it could be heard stretching down the hallway. Will poked his head through the door to examine the area. Just outside the door, a table that had sat between the elevator doors had been turned over, and a small bouquet of flowers sat in the middle of a shattered vase on the floor. When the light flashed, he could see a splatter of blood on the wall above the space where the table looked to have sat, but there wasn't a body anywhere on the ground.

Will drew in a deep breath and then stepped through the doorway.

Almost immediately, he retreated back through the door. He looked back at Brandon, Sam, and Jessica. He held up four fingers, signaling to them that he'd seen at least four Empties lumbering around in the corridor.

"Are they blocking the entire hallway?" Sam whispered.

Will nodded. "But I think I saw the door we've gotta get to. I'm gonna poke my head around the corner and check it out."

"Be careful," Jessica said.

He again moved out of the door and stood with his back flat against the wall. Poking his head around the corner, he saw the Empties again, walking aimlessly in the corridor. One of them seemed to be just walking the width of the hallway, hitting the wall on one side and then turning around again until it reached the opposing wall. Another one walked closer to the end of the hall, and Will could now see a fifth creature walking by. Down at the end of the hall was the door. It seemed so simple a task to reach the door. But navigating the hallway with only a few broomsticks and kitchen knives to rid it of the Empties would be something else completely. Will moved back to the door and looked inside.

"The door is down there, no doubt," he whispered. "But there's no telling how many more of them are in there. I definitely just saw a fifth one walk by, but a lot of the doors appear to be open. For all we know, one of those patient rooms could be filled with the bastards."

"So, what do we do?" Jessica asked.

Will looked across the hallway and saw there were two double doors, similar to the ones upstairs. Behind them, it appeared to be darker than the hallway in front of him, and he assumed there was a very good chance that more Empties would be back there. But he had an idea.

"Wait just a couple of minutes, then make a run for the garage," Will said. "Until then, keep this door shut. Just listen for them."

"What? Where are you going?" Brandon asked.

"Just trust me."

"Will, no," Jessica said. She reached out and grabbed his arm.

He smiled at her. "Don't worry, I'll be fine. Just wait until you don't hear them anymore, and then run like hell."

***

Jessica

Letting go of his arm, Jessica watched as Will stepped into the middle of the hallway. He stopped and looked down toward the beasts, then whistled, and started to wave his arms in the air. She heard the creatures growl, and the sound slowly became increasingly louder. Just out in front of her, Will opened the double doors, then urgently signaled for her to shut the door to the stairway. She did as requested.

"What the fuck is he doing?" Brandon asked.

"He's giving us a clear shot to that door," Sam said.

"I've only seen someone hotwire a car—I've never actually done it," Brandon admitted.

"Well, looks like we're gonna have to figure it out," Jessica said.

She put her ear to the door and listened as the beasts

growled. Closing her eyes to focus, Jessica could almost see them chasing after Will through the double doors. Just as Will had instructed, she waited long enough for the growling of the beasts to fade.

"It sounds like it might be clear," Jessica said.

"You sure? What if there's more of them out there?" Brandon asked.

She shrugged. "Only one way for us to find out."

Jessica reached down and pulled the door open.

Taking her time, she stepped out into the hallway. With the door now open, she could hear the creatures somewhere in the distance, on the other side of the double doors. It sounded to be quite a large group, and Jessica swallowed hard as she wondered if Will was alright. But when she peeked around the corner to look down the main corridor, it appeared vacant. In the flashing light, she could see at least three mangled and motionless figures on the ground between where she stood and the door to the parking garage.

She looked back to Brandon and Sam, who both still stood just inside the door of the stairway. "You ready?"

Brandon nodded nervously and they both stepped out through the door.

Jessica led them, walking cautiously toward the door. As they approached the first body on the floor, she told herself not to look at it. It ranked as some grotesque smell like she'd never experienced in her entire life. The scent alone made her want to turn and throw up, and she wished they had thought about bringing rags to cover their faces. Instead, she cupped her mouth and nose with her hand, holding her broomstick tight in the other. She wanted to close her eyes, so as to help her ignore the body, but she had to keep them open to remain aware of her surroundings.

She couldn't resist looking.

With the body now at her feet, which splashed in a pool of blood, she unconsciously looked down.

It was one of the worst she'd seen. There was hardly anything left, aside from a pile of tattered clothes and a stack of bones. Presumably, the body had been sitting here for over a week, giving the Empties who occupied this floor of the hospital plenty of time to pick it dry. All that remained of the body was a little bit of tissue and muscle. Even the eyes had been gorged—the only thing left on the head, with the exception of some of the skin's underlinings, being the hair. It was the long, kempt hair of a woman. So much blood stained it that she couldn't even tell what color the hair had been, especially with the inconsistent lighting.

She jostled when a hand grabbed her shoulder and then turned to Brandon, who'd used the collar of his t-shirt to cover his face so that he could keep both hands grasped on his makeshift weapon.

"Come on," he said. "Let's keep going." He took the lead, stepping out in front of Jessica and Sam.

A noise sounded from one of the rooms around them, and before Jessica could say anything, something crashed through a door ahead.

Brandon cried out as a large figure wearing a once white overcoat rushed out of the door and grabbed onto him. Brandon instinctively raised his broomstick with both hands, and the Empty took hold of it. They fought each other for leverage and Brandon found himself with his back against the wall, trying to push the beast backward.

Sam lifted his own broomstick and was about to bring it down into the creature when another beast came out of the same room and lunged at him. He turned just in time to get his hands up and block the thing from biting him. They began to struggle near the opposite wall from where Brandon and his assailant fought.

When Jessica took a step toward Brandon in hopes of helping him, she slipped in a pool of blood, falling onto her back and throwing her broomstick behind her in the process. She hit the floor with a thud, and immediately clutched her back. She heard a snap, and looked up to see that Brandon's broomstick had broken. The Empty fell toward him, but Brandon got his hand on its shoulder before it was able to bite him.

"Run!" Brandon shouted.

But Jessica couldn't move. Her eyes, glazed over, happened to come upon one half of Brandon's broomstick, now broken off into a jagged point. She rolled toward it, grasping it as she heard another howl from behind her. Jessica turned toward the door they'd been trying to reach to see two more Empties lumbering toward them.

"Get out of here!" Brandon demanded.

Jessica fought her way onto her hands and knees, then heard a crash, and looked over to see that Brandon and the Empty had fallen. Behind her, the two stragglers approached quickly. Sam had the Empty he'd been fighting pinned against the wall, but was trying to free his hand.

Jessica made her way to one knee, and she felt the strain in her back as she stood all the way up. The pain shooting down her spine caused her to stand with an elderly woman's posture, but she found a way to move and stand over Brandon and his opposition. Just as the creature was about to finally catch hold of the flesh on Brandon's wrist, she drove the stake down into the side of its head, and the grip on Brandon became nonexistent. Jessica fell to the ground again, the execution having taken everything out of her and the pain in her back not subsiding. Brandon breathed heavy, but somehow made it to his feet.

Brandon grabbed the other half of the broomstick off the ground and rushed over to Sam, driving the stake into the head of the creature he'd been fighting. The Empty went limp, and Sam gasped for air.

"Thanks," Sam said.

Brandon turned and delivered a swift kick to one of the approaching beasts, before clutching the other one by the shirt and driving the stake into its eye. It fell to the ground, and Brandon picked up Jessica's unbroken broomstick. The standing Empty let out a scream, and Brandon swung the stick like a baseball bat. The creature didn't even attempt to cover up, and Brandon connected, breaking the stick over the thing's face as it fell to the ground. Brandon was left with a freshly made stake in his hand, and promptly drove it down into the Empty's eye. The fight over, he went down to his knees and gasped for breath.

"Are you okay?" he asked, short on air and looking over at Jessica.

"Yeah," she grimaced. "I took a bad spill, but I'll be fine."

Jessica turned when she heard another crash come from the direction of the elevators. Will appeared at the end of the hall and fell, crawling for a moment before standing upright again. He was waving toward the door to the garage.

"Run! Go!" he shouted.

Behind him, a pack of Empties filled the end of the hall. Too many for Jessica to count.

"Holy shit," Sam said.

Jessica's eyes went wide, and Brandon reached down to pick her up. She grimaced from a shooting pain in her back.

"I'm sorry," Brandon told her. He threw his arm around her and Sam joined from the other side.

"We gotta go, now!" Will shouted, and they headed for the door as the gates of hell seemed to open behind him.

CHAPTER SIX

Will

The growling grew behind them as they raced for the door. Will had almost caught up to them, and wondered what had happened to Jessica to where she now had trouble walking. There'd be time to ask questions later. For now, he just wanted to get them out of the hospital.

When they reached the door to the parking garage, Will looked through a large window to his right and saw a small group of Empties inside a closed room. They slapped the glass with their palms. Reluctantly, he looked back and saw the crowd, fast-approaching them. For the first time, he was able to get a good look at the horde. It had to be made up of at least twenty figures, and they slowed themselves down by grouping from wall to wall, rubbing up against it and fighting for space as they moved toward Will and the others. He heard the hinges on the door in front of him, and saw Brandon using his free hand to push it open.

If the horde hadn't been approaching from behind, Will would have told the anesthesiologist that he should have waited in case something was on the other side. Instead, the door opened, and they were faced with another Empty who'd been trapped.

The Empty lunged at them, and Will stepped in front. He got his stick up just in time to push the creature back, and he moved into the room.

"Come on!" he called back without looking, keeping his eyes focused on the monster in front of him.

The door slammed shut behind him, muffling the calls of the approaching horde. Now the only thing standing between the group and the parking garage was a long-haired Empty wearing turquoise scrubs—probably a former nurse at the hospital who'd been on her way into work when she'd fallen. There were no other bodies in this small room, so the creature must have been trapped here alone for the past week.

"Stay back!" Will called behind him.

The former nurse came at him, and he kicked her in the gut, sending her flying backward. He immediately swung his stick, but the thing's hands were already coming up in front of its face after falling back. The broomstick broke, and Will was left holding only a six-inch piece. He reached to his belt and withdrew the kitchen knife as the Empty stood up straight again.

A crash from behind startled Will, followed by repeated loud banging. The horde inside the hospital had reached the door, and were now slamming themselves against it. Turning back had been a mistake, as the former nurse lunged toward him.

Will saw the panic in Jessica's eyes, and just as she started to point and shout out his name, he turned and thrust the knife toward the creature's head, getting lucky to hit it just above its right eye. The nails on one of its hands scratched Will's arm in the process, but the Empty fell to the ground at Will's feet.

After leaning down and pulling the knife from the monster's head, Will turned back to look at his counterparts. "Ready to keep going?" He had to yell so he could be heard over the constant banging at the door behind them.

Now apparently feeling better, Jessica walked over to Will and slapped him on the arm. He grimaced and put his hand over the burn.

"What was that back there?" Jessica said, anger in her voice.

"We're here, aren't we?" Will said. "You see how many of them there were? There's no way we were going to make it past those things."

"You didn't have to damn near commit suicide!" Jessica shouted.

"She's right, man," Sam said. "That was pretty careless."

Will drew in a deep breath and closed his eyes, shaking his head.

"Come on, guys," Brandon said. "This isn't helping." He looked over to Jessica. "Will's right, we're here." Then he looked over to Will. "But why don't you try to give us a little more of a heads-up next time instead of acting on a whim?"

Will stared at Jessica for a moment and she returned his gaze. Then he looked back to Brandon and nodded.

"Good," Brandon said. "Now, we still have one more door to get through."

Will turned around and walked toward it. There was a sign on the wall next to it that read: "Parking Garage". He pressed his ear to the door, hoping to hear whether there were any Empties on the other side, but the continuous slams on the door behind him prevented him from being able to pinpoint if anything was out there. If they were lucky, the garage would be clear, and they could take a little more time getting a vehicle to start. But luck hadn't exactly been his best friend as of late.

"I'm not sure we're gonna know what's out there without just opening this door," Will said, looking back to them.

"Well, we aren't going back, so I'm not sure it really matters at this point," Brandon replied.

"Right."

Will glanced past them when the door they'd come from made a funny noise. The three of them followed his gaze as well. He looked at the door and noticed it beginning to cave toward them. The Empties on the other side were putting enough force on it to nearly knock it down.

"Time to go," Will said.

Jessica, Sam, and Brandon rushed to the middle of the room, and without hesitation, Will opened the door outward to the parking garage.

***

After stepping out into the garage, Will made sure the door securely shut behind them. He was thankful the knob on the door was round instead of a handle, making it much more unlikely that the creatures would accidentally open it. They'd likely have to crash through it in order to get out to the garage, as they hadn't yet shown the intelligence to do something so simple as turning a door knob.

Screams of the beasts echoed through the garage. Though, to his relief and surprise, this level of the garage was vacant of any creeping shadows. Will wondered if most the creatures who'd been loitering out here had migrated upstairs after the commotion David had caused when he'd fled.

He turned when he heard a loud crash again behind them, and after a few moments, banging started on the door they'd just exited.

"We've gotta hurry," Sam said.

Will scanned the parking garage, and his eyes immediately fell on a Ford Escape twenty yards away from where they stood. Not on the vehicle necessarily, as much as the body he could see sprawled beside it.

"Come on," he called back as he jogged toward the vehicle.

Flies buzzed around the rotted flesh. The corpse wore what was left of a long-sleeve plaid shirt and a pair of khakis. Like the body they'd passed inside the hospital, the bones had been nearly picked clean. It lay in a pool of blood which was infested with small worm-like insects. Will covered his nose to try and mask the smell, but its strength couldn't be ignored. He wondered if he'd ever become accustomed to the smell of the rotting dead, the longer he lived in this new world. He knelt down next to the body just as Jessica, Sam, and Brandon arrived behind him.

"What're you doing?" Jessica asked.

Will ignored her and began rummaging through the dead man's pockets. He also tried to put into the back of his mind what he was doing. The inside of the man's pockets were wet, likely from all the blood. He felt something crawling on his hand and withdrew it quickly to find a small white worm slugging across his knuckles. He slapped at it, then turned and gagged. Behind him, someone threw up, but he didn't look to see who in the group it had been.

The banging at the door grew louder, and Will knew it was only a matter of time before the horde made it through. He reached back into the pockets of the corpse and continued to search for keys to the Escape. Finally, he found them in the breast pocket of the man's shirt after having rolled him over onto his side, and after seeing the man's battered face. It was a strange place for someone to put their keys, but he was thankful to find them. He looked back and flashed them toward the others. Will could tell from the way Brandon wiped his mouth that he was the one who'd vomited.

"Beats the hell out of trying to hotwire it," Will said. "Come on, get in."

Will opened the back door and Jessica jumped in, followed closely by Sam. Brandon ran around to the side of the vehicle and joined Will up front as he turned the key in the ignition. The engine turned over without a fuss, and a stream of static blared through the speakers. Will shut off the stereo with a swipe of his hand and looked at the gas gauge. It was three-quarters of the way full, and he let out a sigh of relief.

Putting the vehicle into reverse, Will backed out of the parking spot and came to a stop with a clear path in front of him. He stared into the rearview mirror.

"What are you waiting on?" Brandon asked. "Go!"

But Will hesitated. "We can't. We have to wait."

Sam put up his arms. "What the hell for?"

"We need to wait on those things to bust out of that door so they follow us out of here. If we don't, we're either gonna have a hell of a time getting back into the hospital when we get back, or they could even join their friends upstairs and bust through *that* door."

Will looked over to Brandon and could see he wasn't sure about the plan. They were silent, and it sounded like the door could come down at any moment. When he looked at it in the mirror, he could see it starting to give.

"He's right," Jessica said. Brandon looked back at her, and Will's gaze went to her in the rearview mirror. "We need to let them get through that door and then ease out of here so they follow us outside. It might even keep them out of the garage for good."

Brandon sighed and looked back to Will. "I hope you're right about this. If the garage fills up in front of us, we're gonna be trapped. Not sure this little thing is gonna be able to pound over too many of them."

Will tightened his grip on the steering wheel, and the monsters roared behind them as the door slammed to the ground.

CHAPTER SEVEN

Gabriel

A clock above the door leading to the garage ticked with every second that passed, and Gabriel eyed it intently. He'd moved a small table out into the main corridor so that he could wait and listen for his friends to return. At the other end of the hall, near the elevators, Holly and Sarah shared a similar task, manning the door to the stairwell in case the four re-entered the hospital from that direction. A shadow caught Gabriel's attention, and he turned to see Marcus setting down a cup of hot tea on the table before sitting down.

They sat in silence for a moment, the ticking clock fighting to be heard above their steadied breaths.

"You think they've even made it out of here yet?" Marcus asked.

"Hope so."

Marcus took no time changing over to a deeper subject. "You still got that same plan of headin' to D.C. once we go and get the boy?"

Gabriel simply nodded.

Marcus took another sip of his tea and was silent.

Gabriel could see in Marcus' eyes that he had more to add, so he decided to ask the next obvious question.

"Why do you ask?"

"I don't know," Marcus said. "Thinkin' of taggin' along if you wouldn't mind."

Gabriel furrowed his brow. "You don't wanna stay here? I assumed you'd all stay in your new little utopia here. Hell, I would if I didn't have a family to get back to, and the responsibility to get Dylan back to his parents."

"Shit, man. Ain't nothin' left for me here. I've lived in Tennessee all my life. And considerin' I'm not sure how much life I got left, I may as well go out and see what else the world has to offer."

Gabriel turned and smiled. "You're not dyin', man. Not anytime soon."

"Come pretty close the last few days. Shit gets you thinkin', ya know?"

Thinking about his downtrodden relationship with his wife, Gabriel knew exactly what Marcus meant. If he died before finding his family, his final emotion would be regret. And if he made it to Washington and couldn't find them—or worse, discovered them either dead or turned Empty—he wasn't quite sure how he'd live with himself. He'd tried not to think too much about either of those two scenarios, but times like these where he had little to do but swim in his thoughts made it all the more difficult not to ponder what *could* be awaiting him.

"Alright," Gabriel said. "I'm gonna run to my room for a few minutes, then we can go gather the bodies."

Marcus nodded. "Go do your thing, brother."

Gabriel patted Marcus on the back, then stood.

On the way to his room, he tried to think of other things he could do to procrastinate having to go move Will's mother.

***

Jessica

As the vehicle eased forward, Jessica kept an eye on the large group lumbering behind them, allowing Will to stay focused on getting them out of the parking garage. So far, Will's plan was going off without a hitch. He'd turned a corner to head down to the next level of the garage, and the creatures had followed.

"This speed is perfect," she said. "They're coming after us like they think they're gonna catch us."

"But we're not gonna let that happen," Brandon said, presenting it almost like a question.

"Not planning on it," Will said. "But maybe if they do, you can jump out and distract 'em for us."

Jessica smiled, but Brandon didn't find it funny, narrowing his eyes.

As they passed the third level, Jessica watched another small group of Empties join the existing horde. If Will had driven past a few moments later, this new group would have been blocking the way in front of them.

"Hey, I think your plan garnered the attention of their friends," Jessica said.

"Good," Will said. "Hopefully that'll make for a clearer path when we get back."

They reached the exit unscathed. The fire truck Will's group had come to the hospital in still sat in the same spot they'd parked it.

"Looks like the tires are blown out," Will said, speaking of the fire truck.

"David must've shot 'em on his way out," Sam said.

Jessica looked ahead as Will exited the well-lit garage and entered the pitch black darkness of the night. He was finally forced to turn the headlights on. When he did, three Empties appeared in the beams, standing just yards away from the hood of the SUV. He tried to swerve, but ended up hitting one of them. A second creature slammed its hands on the hood while another banged against the glass. Jessica looked back and saw the oncoming horde approaching fast.

"Go!" Brandon yelled.

Will hesitated. "I've gotta make sure this group follows me."

The Empty screamed, continuing to pound on the glass. Jessica had remained calm and trusted Will this entire time, but now even she was becoming nervous. She looked back again and saw the group getting closer. The SUV began to shake, and she looked to the side of the vehicle to see the three beasts pushing against it.

"Will," Jessica said with a tremble, "I think he's right—we need to—"

"Just trust me," Will said, cutting her off.

The Escape crept forward again, and one of the Empties banged on the window immediately beside Jessica. The creature had once been a woman, and was somehow still wearing radiant red hair and an open blouse. Will eased out into the street, and another two Empties came up from the other side of the car. They'd apparently been wandering down the sidewalk and been drawn in by the commotion. Jessica could feel the sweat form on her brow. She became distractingly wet under her arms and on her palms, and she rubbed her knees nervously, an old habit she'd had since middle school.

"Tell me when the entire group is out of the garage," Will said, speaking to any of the three in the car who might still be listening to him and not the creatures.

It was hard to be sure with no light behind them, and with just trying to see past the glowing eyes of the approaching horde, but Jessica couldn't see anymore creatures within the lighting of the garage.

"It looks clear," she said.

Glancing back at her through the rearview mirror, Will asked, "You sure?"

"Positive," she lied.

She jolted back against the seat as Will punched the gas. Out of the corner of her eye, Jessica saw the Empty who'd been knocking on the door beside her fall. Will drove another thirty yards before slamming on the breaks and turning the car a hundred and eighty degrees. The lights faced the horde now, who seemed to be walking faster now to try and reach the SUV.

"I think you've led them far enough," Brandon said. "Please, go."

Jessica leaned up and put her hand on Will's shoulder.

"Come on," she whispered. "Let's get out of here before we push our luck. They're not gonna go back into that garage. They're gonna continue to follow us, even when we're long gone."

Will hesitated, then finally turned the vehicle around.

Jessica leaned back and quietly sighed. She understood the intention in Will's plan, and it was smart. But the way he'd gone about it still felt a touch reckless. Brandon sat in the front seat with his arms crossed, and he looked like he'd lost his patience with Will altogether.

In minutes, they were pulling onto the ramp for I-40, headed for Brandon's dad's house.

CHAPTER EIGHT

Will

Brandon's father, Jack Nix, owned a house on the western outskirts of Knoxville. It wasn't the same house Brandon had grown up in; his mother still resided in that house. They'd divorced on the tail end of Brandon's teenage years when he'd just turned twenty. So his father, a hard-working independent contractor, had bought a small ranch-style home on a couple of acres, giving him at least a little space from his neighbors.

When they arrived at the road Jack lived on, the lights in most of the houses were off. The street lights were no longer on, and Will assumed that they must have lost power in the neighborhood. Two houses had small gleams of light on the inside, likely drawing power from generators. No Empties appeared to be in the street, but Will had the headlights turned off so as to not draw any attention. Through the silence, they could hear that there were indeed beasts out there somewhere, but they didn't sound to be too close. Thankfully, the moon was full and provided them with a little bit of light, though Will could still barely see beyond a few yards in front of the car.

"We're almost there. It's just up here on the right," Brandon said.

Easing the car forward, Will's heart raced. He had a

feeling that one of the creatures would jump out in front of the small SUV at any moment, but it had yet to happen, leaving him all the more on edge. Sweat surrounded the perimeter of his hands on the steering wheel as he waited for Brandon to tell him they'd arrived.

"Slow down," Brandon said, "the driveway's right here."

Will saw the entrance to the driveway and eased the car into it. The outline of the house appeared and Will tapped the brakes just as they approached the garage. He put it into park, and then they sat quietly and listened for Empties surrounding the area.

After a few moments, Jessica whispered, "Sounds clear."

Will looked over to Brandon. "So, what's the plan? Do you have a key?"

Shaking his head, Brandon said, "Not on me. Left that at my house." He looked back toward his father's home. "I think we should go around the back just in case any of the neighbors are still home. People around here are pretty damn protective, and I know they'd look out for my old man's shit."

"Sounds like a plan," Will said.

"What do you want me to do?" Sam asked.

"Stand outside the car and keep a look out," Will said.

Sam nodded.

"Hope his place hasn't already been raided," Will said.

"Only one way to find out," Jessica said, and Will heard her door click open.

Leaving the key in the ignition, Will pulled the handle and joined Jessica outside. He grabbed her by the arm.

"I think you should stay in here."

"Why?" Jessica asked.

"Because one of us needs to keep the car running. You already have a hurt shoulder, so it makes sense for you to be ready to get us the hell out of here. Sam can stand outside and keep a look-out."

"Alright," Jessica said, sighing.

"If either of you see or hear anything strange, honk the horn three times," Will said.

"Roger that," Sam said.

Will turned to head behind the house, and Jessica called his name. He looked back to face her.

"Don't do anything stupid in there," Jessica said.

Will shook his head. "I won't."

***

Empties howled off in the distance. Will could even hear them shuffling through the fields behind Jack's house, but creatures didn't appear to be an immediate threat. The windows and door at the back of the house were still intact and looked untouched—a good sign that no one had raided the place yet.

Brandon walked over and tried to turn the handle to the back door, but it was locked.

"No surprise there," he said.

Will looked to the houses on either side of them and saw that they were shrouded in darkness. The closest house with lights on was three houses down on the other side of the street. What made him most nervous were the Empties that he could hear in the distance behind the house.

"We're gonna have to be quick," Will said. "Those things don't sound too far away. Is there a ditch or anything back

64

there that would prevent them from getting to us?"

"No," Brandon said. "It's a clear path. All that land is undeveloped."

"Do you know exactly where he keeps his guns?"

"Yeah, he's got a case back in his bedroom."

Will drew in a deep breath. A shovel leaned against the wall next to him and he grabbed it.

"Well, I hope so," Will said. "'Cause there's no easy way to do this, and we're definitely going to attract attention."

He lifted the shovel up onto his shoulder, almost like a baseball bat.

"Ready?"

Brandon drew in his own deep breath. "Yeah, I guess."

On that mark, Will reared back and swung the shovel into the window, shattering the glass on the first try. The sound was deafening. Their clock began to tick.

Brandon reached through the window and unlocked the door. He opened it, and the two men headed inside.

***

Jessica

Jessica turned around, looking to other houses on the street to see if anyone had heard the window break. Everything looked the same, but she now worried that any Empties in the area would have been attracted by the crash and be heading toward the house. They'd heard some of the creatures when they'd come from the end of the street, so they knew there were some lurking around, though she couldn't hear any now.

"Everything okay, Sam?" she whispered.

Sam poked his head through the passenger side window.

"So far, so good."

She turned her wrist over, gripping the steering wheel tight.

"Please, hurry," she mumbled under her breath.

***

Will

Directly on the other side of the back door was the kitchen, and Will found himself standing on the tile floor near a granite top island that reflected the moon's light coming in from a window above the sink. He awaited Brandon's lead.

"Come on, his bedroom is back this way."

Will followed Brandon through the living room, running into the back of the sofa and nearly falling. He stopped to gather himself, gripping the top of the couch as he guided himself around it.

Brandon hadn't waited on Will, and a door swung open in the hallway, its knob slamming into the adjacent wall.

Brandon screamed.

"Brandon!"

Will let go of the sofa and ran toward the hallway. Paying no attention to his unfamiliar surroundings, he tripped over a coffee table in the middle of the room and stumbled onto the floor. He braced himself with his hands, grimacing when all his weight fell onto the bandaged hand he'd punched the mirror with earlier. Still, adrenaline pumped through him and he jumped to his feet, running toward the direction of the scream.

When he reached the end of the hallway, Will came to an open room. Inside, he saw Brandon sitting on the carpet with his back against a dresser. One of his hands covered his mouth as his shoulders shuddered, and he stared up at something on the other side of the room. Will crept closer until he was through the doorway, and his gaze followed Brandon's.

"Oh, shit."

A man sat upright against a headboard on a king size bed. What remained of his head had slumped to his shoulder. A large handgun lay beside him, suggesting he'd died from a self-inflicted gunshot wound. Will looked back down to Brandon, who sniffled as tears ran down to his hand on his face.

"I thought he was in Florida," Brandon mumbled. "I had no idea he'd even be here."

The man on the bed was Jack Nix, Brandon's father, dead of an apparent suicide.

Kneeling down, Will rubbed Brandon's shoulder and didn't reply. There were no words he could say. He knew that firsthand, having just lost both his parents in just a matter of days.

From outside Will heard a scream, and he turned back toward the rear of the house. It was inhuman—that much he knew. The Empties were inching closer.

"Brandon, I know this is hard, but we need to get as much out of this case as we can and get the hell out of here."

Looking down at the ground, Brandon wept into his hand. Will didn't waste anymore time. He slipped over to the closet and opened it. Rummaging past shoes, he found the strap to a duffle bag and pulled it out.

Near the bed stood a large cherry wood gun case, one of

its doors still open. He hurried over to it and started to empty ammunition and hand guns into the bag. He also found a holster, tossing that into the duffle as well. He threw a rifle over each shoulder, and pulled out three shotguns. Placing the shotguns on the bed along with the bag, he pulled out a box of shells and loaded each weapon. He kept his focus, fighting not to let his gaze move toward Mr. Nix. The smell in the air was horrendous, but he was too set on gathering the firearms and getting out of the house to worry about it.

Once the shotguns were loaded, he went back to Brandon and kneeled down.

"Brandon, we have to go, dude."

But Brandon didn't budge.

Another howl came from outside, this time followed by a collection of them, and Will shook Brandon's face.

"Now! We've gotta get out of here!"

Brandon finally seemed to snap out of it. Trembling, he nodded toward Will and took his hand to stand up.

"Take these, I can get the rest," Will said, and he put two of the shotguns into Brandon's chest. Will walked back over to the bed and threw the duffle bag over his shoulder and grabbed the last shotgun before he headed out into the hallway, making his way into the living room.

Will peeked out the window next to the front door to make sure it was clear. He could make out Jessica's silhouette in the driver's seat. His hand went to the deadbolt and he turned it.

"Alright, let's get..."

When Will turned around, he saw Brandon walking to the

center of the living room, facing the back door. Outside, a horde of Empties approached the house from the field.

"Oh, shit," Will said. "We gotta go, now!"

But Brandon ignored him and started walking toward the back door. As he walked, he pumped the shotgun.

"What are you doing?" Will asked, but Brandon ignored him. Will hurried over and put his hand on Brandon's shoulder, who reared back his elbow and caught Will in the side of the face. Will fell back onto the ground, dropping the shotgun, and reached up to feel for blood. Brandon looked down on him. They were in a part of the room where the moonlight peeked in from the kitchen, and Will could see the shadow behind Brandon's eyes.

"Get the fuck out of here," Brandon told him. His voice was calm and collected. He placed one of the shotguns on a table beside him and turned his back toward Will again. He started for the back door.

Will jumped to his feet. "Brandon, wait!"

Brandon turned around and fired a round into the sofa beside Will. The sound was deafening, and Will fell back onto the ground, covering his ears.

"Get the fuck out of here!" Brandon yelled. "I won't fucking miss next time!"

Will's eyes widened as he came to the realization of what was going on. Brandon had snapped, and there was no turning back. Will could either try to save him and die in the process, or he could abandon him, as he was being asked to do.

The front door opened and Sam came rushing inside.

"What's going on? I heard a shot," Sam said.

"Get out of here, Sam," Brandon said.

Will leaned over to Sam and whispered. "His father is dead in the other room. He's lost it."

Brandon reached the back door, the Empties now just twenty yards away from the patio. He looked back to Will, and he had tears in his eyes now.

"Go," Brandon mumbled.

Will turned to leave, but Sam took a step toward Brandon.

Will narrowed his eyes. "Come on, Sam. We can't save him."

"I'm not leaving him," Sam said. He brought his hand to his chest and pulled away the collar of his shirt. The moon let in just enough light at this angle to illuminate the cut on Sam's shoulder blade. "It's small, but that son of a bitch at the hospital got me."

Will's eyes widened.

Brandon went to the other side of the room and grabbed the extra shotgun off of the nearby table. He confirmed it was loaded, then threw it to Sam.

"You guys can't do this!" Will pleaded.

Brandon kicked down the back door, and the howls of the Empties rang into the house. Will grabbed the shotgun and jumped to his feet again, then raced for the front door. He heard the pump of the shotgun and looked back to see Brandon take the first shot, smoke filling the air around the barrel as he connected with one of the beasts outside.

"Go, Will," Sam said. "Just go." He then turned toward the back door, pumping the shotgun.

Hands shaking, Will opened the front door and ran

outside.

***

Jessica

"Get out here," Jessica mumbled.

The gunshot had drawn Sam inside, taking away her eyes outside of the vehicle. Moments earlier, she'd heard the creatures approaching from behind the house, and she now found herself looking around to see if any Empties had gathered in the front yard. She'd even slumped in the seat to try and hide in case any showed up.

A bang came from the back yard and Jessica's tired eyes widened. Almost simultaneously, the front door swung open and Jessica sat up straight in the seat. Carrying a rifle on each shoulder, a large bag, and a shotgun in his hands, Will ran to the vehicle. He opened the passenger-side back door and tossed the weapons on the seat, slammed the door, and then jumped into the seat next to Jessica.

"Go!" Will yelled.

Jessica narrowed her eyes. "No, wait. Where's Brandon and Sam?"

A gut-wrenching scream came from the backyard, and it caught both Will and Jessica's gaze. Jaw dropped, Jessica looked over to Will.

"It's too late," Will said. "Get us out of here. I'll explain on the way."

Her hands trembling, Jessica grabbed the shift, put the car into reverse, and backed out of the driveway. She pulled into the street unscathed, and started to creep down the road.

"Turn on the lights," Will said. "No reason to try and hide

anymore. Just get us the hell out of this place."

Jessica turned the lever to shine the headlights, and her eyes widened again. There was a narrow path in front of them down the middle of the road, but it was quickly filling with Empties.

"Shit! Go!" Will yelled.

But Jessica's foot was already on the gas.

Around them, the beasts growled and lunged toward them. Nails scratched at the sides of the SUV, but Jessica managed to move past the small horde to an open road. A house with lights on on the inside caught Jessica's gaze and she looked to see a young girl standing in a window upstairs. The child held a stuffed animal close to her chest and waved at Jessica as they passed.

Jessica faced her head back to the road and turned onto the main throughway without stopping as she reached the end of the street.

CHAPTER NINE

Will

When they had almost arrived back at the hospital, Will was sure to remind Jessica to pull into the garage from the opposite direction they'd left. His hope was that the Empties they'd led out of the garage had continued to aimlessly follow them down the street and had now disappeared far off into the city and the night.

"Cut the lights," Will said. The working street lamps along the sidewalk could guide them, and Will hoped turning the headlights off would help keep them from attracting Empties.

As they arrived at the side of the hospital, just around the corner from the entrance to the parking garage, Will was honestly surprised to not see any Empties yet. Normally, at least a few of the things hung around each side of the building. When they turned the corner, it was much the same. There was a large spot of light on the road that shined from the parking garage, and there still didn't seem to be any creatures around.

"You really think they all left?" Jessica asked.

"Hopefully. Just gotta be on the lookout in the garage."

Will didn't say it, but he hoped to God that the creatures hadn't turned around and headed back to the top of the parking garage. His worst fear was that they'd reach the door leading back to the group, but that it would have been busted down, and the place overrun with Empties.

Jessica pulled the Ford Escape into the entrance of the garage, and Will cracked his window. If any Empties were in here, their snarls would echo through the open concrete space.

But he didn't hear anything.

With each level they moved up in the garage, a feeling of relief passed over Will. There wasn't a single Empty in sight, and he was still unable to hear any.

As they inched closer to the top level, he finally began to hear snarls. But when they came around the last corner and headed up the small incline, just two beasts stood at the top, near the door.

"They must've not felt like following their friends out of here," Jessica said. "You gonna shoot 'em?"

Will shook his head. "We don't know how far those others made it. A gun shot in the garage will sound off a long way. Plus, I really don't want to scare anyone inside."

"Alright, so what do you wanna do?"

Will pushed the button to lower the window the rest of the way and he hung his head out the door. Putting his fingers to his lips, he whistled. The two creatures turned to face the vehicle, and they snarled louder.

"What are you doing?" Jessica asked.

The Empties walked toward the small SUV, standing almost shoulder to shoulder with each other.

"Hit the gas," Will said.

She looked at him and narrowed her eyes. "And mess up a car we have keys to? No!"

He ignored her. "Wait just a second. Let them get past where the fence used to be."

"I'm not going to hit them."

"Yes you are. We don't need this car. There's plenty others here if this one gets wrecked."

The two Empties walked past where the gate had once stood, and Will pointed toward them.

"Now!"

Jessica hit the gas, and the front end plowed into the two creatures, sending one over the top of the vehicle and cracking the windshield in the process. The other creature went under one of the tires.

Will opened the glove box and grabbed the large kitchen knife he'd stored in there; then, he stepped out of the car.

He went to the beast closest to the vehicle. It lay on its back, and one of its legs had been almost severed. This one had gone under the vehicle. It didn't even put up a fight as Will leaned down and stabbed the knife into the side of its head.

The other Empty sat up, and Will kicked it in the shoulder as he approached it, driving the knife down into its forehead. He hurried back to the vehicle and got inside.

"Pull up close to the door," Will said. He looked over to Jessica, who was staring at him, a look of concern over her face. "What?"

"Do you feel any remorse when you kill them?" she asked.

Will shook his head. "They aren't human. Not anymore."

"But you still have to look into those eyes when you kill them."

"Their eyes are empty, and I have to stay convinced of

that. If I start trying to tell myself there's a person back there, I'll hesitate. If I hesitate, I'll die."

He used a towel that he found in the glove box to wipe down the blade of the knife.

Jessica bowed her head.

"What?" Will asked.

"I'm just worried we're going to lose all our humanity," Jessica said. "That we're all gonna become dark and cold."

He lifted her chin so she'd look at him and then said, "Everything we're doing is to save whatever humanity we have left. That's why we're here. Guys like David Ellis, I'm sure there's a lot of them out there. People who've already let go of any dignity they had. But that's not gonna be us."

Without saying another word, Jessica eased off the brake and pulled the car toward the door.

***

Gabriel

"They're back!"

The shout in the hall came from Holly, and Gabriel rose out of bed and rubbed his eyes. After he and Marcus had gathered the bodies of Melissa, Kristen, and Trevor, he'd tried to lay down for a little while. It had been useless, as he'd had far too much on his mind to grab any sleep.

Gabriel stepped out of his room to see Will coming through the door at the end of the hall. Marcus took a bag from Will as Will set a shotgun and a rifle on a nearby table. Will's hands were red and his clothes were soaked in blood. Holly ran to him and he held her tight. She was crying, and Will gave her long strokes up and down her back, assuring her he was fine.

When Jessica walked in just after Will, she shut the door behind her, then set down a rifle she'd had in her hands. Gabriel's eyes narrowed. Sarah came from her room and walked past Gabriel, and she was able to get the question out before he could.

"Where's Brandon and Sam?" Sarah asked.

Will pulled back from Holly and looked at Sarah. It was a familiar look, and Gabriel knew right away—just from Will's eyes—that the news wouldn't be good. Will glanced over to Marcus with tired eyes, then looked back to Sarah and shook his head.

"I'm sorry," Will said.

"Sorry for what?" Sarah asked quizzically.

Will lowered his head, placing his hands on his hips.

Sarah covered her mouth and started to cry, and Holly left Will's side to go to her. Holly wrapped her arm around the nurse, then led her down the hallway to her room.

Gabriel made his way over to Will, Marcus, and Jessica, and he reached out to shake Will's bloody hand, pulling him in for an embrace.

"Glad you made it back," Gabriel said as they patted each other's backs. He pulled away.

"What happened to them?" Marcus asked.

"I really need to sit down," Will told them, collapsing down at a nearby table.

Gabriel listened as Will first explained to them the good news about how his strategy to lead the Empties out of the garage had worked, making it a breeze to get back into the hospital when they'd returned. Will then told them everything that had happened at the house, and how

Brandon had eroded once he'd found his father lying in his bed, dead of an apparent suicide.

"I tried to get him out of there, but he fired a shotgun at me. Told me if I didn't leave him, he wouldn't miss the next time. Sam ran inside once he heard the gunshot. He decided to stay with Brandon. We ran into some resistance on our way out to the parking garage, and he got bit."

"Shit," Marcus said.

Will bowed his head. "There was a large horde that had made it to the back patio, but I still shouldn't have left them."

Gabriel started to say something, but before he could, Jessica spoke.

"I would have done the same thing after I found my parents if your mom hadn't been there to talk some sense into me. But I wanted to live. Brandon made his choice."

"And you can't blame Sam for what he did," Marcus added.

Will looked up and nodded, and then his eyes met Gabriel's. "How'd everything go here?"

"We've got everything ready to go," Gabriel said. "Just take your time getting cleaned up and we can start whenever you're ready."

Will squeezed Gabriel's shoulder. "Thanks, brother." Will stood up, then leaned down to kiss Jessica on the forehead and mumbled, "Thank you."

He left for his room.

***

Will

The rest of the group were awaiting Will when he came back out of his room about a half hour later. Holly stood at the front and, without a word, took Will's hand as he approached her. She turned and walked with him down the long hallway toward the elevators as the rest of the group followed. Everyone was silent.

As they reached the elevators, they turned to the double doors which were now decorated with flowers. Holly would later mention that she'd collected them from the various vases that sat around the hospital. Gabriel moved in front of them and finally broke the silence.

"You ready?" he asked, looking at Will.

Will drew in a deep breath. He knew what lay on the other side of the doors. It had been the hardest day of his entire life, and he hoped this makeshift ceremony could bring some kind of closure. He looked to Gabriel and nodded. As Gabriel moved to open the doors, Will's grip on Holly's hand tightened. She returned the gesture, stroking the top of his hand with her index finger.

Gabriel pushed open the doors, and there they lay.

The four bodies had been placed on the ground, each covered with a white sheet. Their only identifiers were pieces of paper neatly placed on each of them, the given victim's name handwritten in a beautiful script.

The first in line was Rachel, the hospital receptionist who David had thrown into the room with the hospital's experiment Empty, forcing her to let the creature loose. When she'd tried to escape after her task was complete, David had shot her in the leg so that she couldn't get away. The rest of the group had had to listen and watch as the Empty had devoured her.

Next to her was Kristen, the innocent nurse who David

had killed in his attempt to show Rachel and the rest of the group that he wasn't bluffing. Will sensed that everyone in the group knew that it could have been any of them lying there; Kristen had just so happened to be the unlucky person standing next to David when he'd decided to pull the trigger just to prove a point.

Trevor lay adjacent to Kristen, his body having been retrieved from the area where the group had stored their weapons. From what Jessica had overheard, he'd been stabbed after he'd helped the two rednecks and David with stealing all their weapons.

Will's eyes moistened as he looked at the last body in the line, and Holly shifted in reaction to the new tension from him, going from clutching his hand to wrapping her arm around him.

Though he couldn't see her face, Melissa Kessler, Will's mother, lay under the third sheet, her name beautifully written across a piece of paper placed on her chest. Marcus held the door opposite Gabriel, and Will, Holly, and Sarah stepped through.

Marcus stepped forward, moving to the other side of the bodies so he could face the group.

"Would anyone like to say anything?" Marcus asked.

After another few moments of silence, Sarah stepped forward, wiping her eyes, and began to talk about Kristen. Working as nurses on the same floor of the hospital, the two women had worked together often and become close. Sarah spoke about the first time she'd met Kristen. It had been her first day in the hospital, and Kristen had been on the same shift. Sarah shadowed Kristen most of the day, and they'd sat down and had their first lunch together, as well. This had been less than a year ago, and now Kristen was gone.

She tried to gather herself to talk about Rachel and Trevor, but she was too distraught. She had to step out of the room.

All eyes seemed to fall on Will after Sarah departed. He had barely paid attention to what Sarah had said about the other two women, focused solely on his mother. It pained him that he couldn't see her. How was he supposed to get closure if he couldn't actually see what lay under the sheet? His gaze finally left the body and he looked around to see the rest of the group looking at him in silence. He hoped they didn't expect him to speak, as no words came to him.

"Melissa Kessler was an amazing woman."

Will looked to the side and saw Jessica staring at him. She stepped forward and stood next to Marcus.

"While I didn't know her long, she became almost like another mother to me over the short time we did spend together. She was one of the strongest women I've ever met." She cleared her throat, and her eyes never left Will's. He got lost in them, listening intently as she spoke. "When Walt died, I thought I was going to lose her, too. She was devastated. She loved your dad so much. But she was too strong to give up. I could tell it wasn't in her nature. She was determined to find you, Will, and even though her death was premature, I think she died in peace, knowing that you were alive."

Will's eyes gave way as tears poured from them. Jessica came over, and Will felt Holly let go as Jessica embraced him. She lay her head on his chest and he held her tight.

His red eyes looked down past Jessica to his mother's body, and he saw David Ellis' face in the stark white sheets.

CHAPTER TEN

<u>Dylan</u>

When Dylan's eyes opened again, he was surprised to find that his hands were free. He immediately grabbed his wrists, rubbing down the grotesque wounds that the chains had embedded into them.

He lay on his back and stared up to a ceiling fan. It spun and whistled, sending a cool breeze down upon him. Rolling over toward a wall, he felt the surface he was lying on. They'd placed him on an old mattress on the floor, its sheets stained and unwashed. He could have complained about it, but he was just relieved to have his hands free of the shackles and not be trapped in the dank barn.

"Are you okay?"

The voice startled Dylan, and he turned to see a young girl. She appeared to be around his age, with long dark hair and bright green eyes, and she wore a tattered dress.

"I'm sorry I scared you," the girl said. She was lying down, but sat up straight on her mattress to talk to him. Like Dylan's, her mattress lay on the wood floor, though her sheets appeared to be a little bit cleaner than his. "My name's Mary Beth."

"I-I'm Dylan." His jaw ached when he spoke, the gag having spent hours in his mouth. He worked to stretch it, opening it and closing it a few times. Even talking felt strange to him, and his own voice sounded almost unfamiliar.

Mary Beth smiled. "Hi Dylan."

He looked around the room. It appeared old and unkempt, train engine wallpaper torn away from the drywall in several spots. In one corner of the room he saw cobwebs, and on the wall near him, there were five wooden letters hanging on the wall that read "BRIAN", though the "R" looked like it might fall off the wall at any moment, hanging at an awkward angle.

"Where am I?" Dylan asked.

Before Mary Beth could answer, the door swung open, the knob slamming against the wall behind it. Two people appeared in the doorway: a man and a woman. The burly man had a large beard and long hair coming over the V of his tank top. The woman had stringy brown hair and a toothless grin, though she appeared to only be in her 30's—seemingly far too young to worry about porcelain teeth unless you have a career as a professional hockey player. He realized he recognized both of them from when he'd first been brought to the farm. They'd both been there when he'd been dragged out of the trunk, and the woman had even been the one to blindfold him.

The man picked Dylan up before the boy could protest, and dragged him out into a hallway.

"Don't hurt him!" Mary Beth cried, but the woman slammed the door behind them.

"Where are you taking me?" asked Dylan, but neither of the adults responded.

Their feet creaked on the wooden floor as the large man

carried the boy to a restroom down the hall. The man placed Dylan on his feet in the middle of the bathroom.

"Strip," the large man said.

Dylan looked down at his tattered clothes, crying now, and failed to do as the man asked.

Apparently impatient, the man leaned down and tore at Dylan's clothes as the woman watched. He ripped off the shirt, unbuttoned the boy's pants and yanked them off, and then tore away his underwear, leaving the pre-teen child stark naked in front of the two strangers, his face red with embarrassment.

Not even bothering to ask Dylan to get in himself, the man picked him up again and put him in the bathtub before he turned on the showerhead.

The cold water poured down and stung Dylan's skin. He yelled out, begging the man or woman to warm the water, but neither listened. Dylan tried to shield himself from the water, but it was useless. He looked down and saw the water turning a light brown—not surprising considering how long it had been since he'd had a shower.

After a few moments, he looked up to see the woman leaning in.

"Stay still," she commanded.

She grabbed a bar of soap and lathered his entire body. When the soap was all over him, she used an old body brush, far too rough to be used on human skin, to scrub him with.

"You're hurting me!" he cried out, but the woman continued to rub him down with the brush like she was trying to grind the rust off of an old coin. He swung his hands, slapping the woman on the arms. She grimaced and slapped him across his face.

"Keep that shit up, and I'm gonna let him bathe you," the woman said, signaling back to the large man. "And believe me, you don't want that."

Dylan finally conceded, knowing that crying wasn't going to do him any good. In fact, his resistance had only made the woman scrub harder.

She shut off the cold water and Dylan found himself shivering. She put a towel over him that was more like a rag, barely large enough to cover his shoulders, and started drying him. She used almost as much force as she had with the brush, not allowing him to dry himself.

When she was done, the man came back and picked Dylan up under his arms. Dylan squealed, his arms still sore from the chains they'd hung him from in the barn.

The man lowered Dylan back to the ground, and he noticed the used clothes hanging over the sink.

"Put these on," the man said.

Dylan abided, having no interest in finding out what would happen if he refused to put on the dirty clothes. The shirt was two sizes too big, but the elastic band sweatpants fit just fine. He didn't want to think about where the underwear had come from, so he just slipped it on, trying to convince himself that it was his own.

When he was finished, the woman grabbed him by the arm, pinching him, and led him back down to the bedroom.

The man opened the door and the woman pushed him inside. Somehow, he managed not to fall, and the door was slammed and locked behind him.

Dylan looked over to see Mary Beth on her bed. She sat

with her knees to her chin, not even glancing his way.

"Where am I?" he asked her, but the girl didn't respond. "Mary Beth?"

She looked over to him, tears coming from her eyes, and shook her head.

"Why won't you talk to me?"

Mary Beth turned away from him and looked to the wall next to her.

Confused, Dylan went to his own bed to lie down. He noticed that, while they still weren't exactly new, the sheets had been changed to something cleaner than what had been there before.

Dylan fell on his belly, and all he could do was cry, thinking about how much he missed Gabriel and his friends.

***

A door slamming combined with yelling from down the hall awoke Dylan. He shot up off his stomach and went onto all fours before sitting up straight in a mound of blankets. He looked around the room and didn't see the girl.

"Mary Beth?"

The door opened and Dylan backed up against the wall.

Two people walked in. It was the woman who'd helped him in the shower earlier and a man he remembered as one of the men who'd been there when he'd been kidnapped.

The man walked to the end of the bed and the woman stood behind him. He smacked his gums, chewing on something that brought a fowl stench into the room. The smacking drew Dylan's attention to the man's teeth, which had mostly a yellow tint, and the hair around his mouth looked to be discolored as well.

Looking down at Dylan, the man scoffed. "What you scared of, boy? Look around." He waved his arms and scanned the filthy, dank room. "We put you in the suite!"

"Where's Mary Beth?" Dylan mumbled.

"Oh, she's fine. Don't you worry 'bout her. She's getting all bathed up, just like you did."

Trembling, Dylan said, "I wanna go home."

The man laughed. "Home? What's wrong with here?"

"I want my mom," Dylan said.

"Where's home, kid?"

Dylan bowed his head and didn't reply.

"Now, Dylan, I'm trying to be your friend here, buddy," he said.

"How do you know my name?"

"Well, our friend, Mary Beth, told us."

"She's not your friend. She told me so."

"She must have been joking around, then!" The man was smiling. "Mary Beth loves us!"

"I don't believe you," mumbled Dylan.

The man laughed and looked back at the woman behind him. "You know what, Cindy? You know why he's scared of us?"

"Why?" she asked, keeping a stern look on her face.

"'Cause he doesn't know our names! We're just strangers to him 'til he knows our names."

He looked back toward Dylan, then sat on the edge of the bed. Dylan tried to scoot away further, but he was already against the wall and in the corner. He had nowhere else to go.

"My name's Clint, and this here is Cindy."

"Did you hurt Gabriel?" Dylan asked.

"That the guy who was with you when we found you?" Clint smiled. "Oh, I think Gabriel is coming to see you real soon!"

"I don't believe you."

Footsteps bellowed from the hallway, and another man walked into the room. It was the large man who had helped Cindy bathe him. He held a plate in his hand. Steam rose from the top, and a knife and fork hung off the edge of it.

"Dinnertime already?" Clint asked, turning around. "Can you believe that, Cindy? Time just flies on by!"

The smell hit Dylan's nose and his stomach growled at the beauty of it. Meals had been scarce on the road with his new friends, and he hadn't eaten anything since he'd been brought here except for bread and some kind of nasty chocolate drink they'd poured down his throat. He could practically taste the juicy steak on the tip of his lips, which he tried to wet.

Clint looked back to the boy. "Well, I hoped to have you down for dinner with us. Gonna be a good one. Cooked up a lot of steak, right off the grill. Got some potatoes, freshly picked corn. Ya know, all the good stuff. But, I guess you're not interested in all that, seeing's how you don't wanna become friends with us."

Clint stood up, and Dylan finally came out of his ball.

"Wait, wait. What do you want to know? I'm starving!"

"Sorry, kid. Too late for that," Clint said, turning his back.

"Please!" Dylan started to cry. "Please, I'm so hungry."

But Clint had already left the room, and so had the man with the steak, though the meat had left its impact on the room.

Cindy walked to the door, and just before she walked out, she reached into her pocket. She pulled out a can and tossed it to Dylan.

It fell on the bed in front of him, and he looked down to see another one of the off-brand chocolate protein shakes.

"Wait!" Dylan cried.

But the door was already shut, the lock grinding into place to seal him inside.

CHAPTER ELEVEN

Will

When the sun rose the next morning, Will lay in bed, eyes wide open, staring at the ceiling. The night had come and gone, and he'd hardly slept—maybe an hour, at most. Holly lay next to him, still resting peacefully. She'd fallen asleep with her arm over his chest, but at first chance, he'd moved her off to the side. He wasn't in the mood to be touched; there was far too much on his mind. He could feel his back was stiff, he having stayed still on the firm bed for most of the night. It was an easier position to gather his thoughts in, and he'd known that he wouldn't be able to fall asleep while lying on his back.

He swung his feet over the side of the bed, and as he sat upright, the ache in his back came alive. He let out a groan as he arched back. Then leaning over to touch his toes, Will could feel every inch of the strain on his backside. After about two minutes bent over, the pain began to subside, and he stood up straight again—slowly, so as to not throw his back all the way out. He needed coffee. A t-shirt and a pair of shorts lay over a chair against the wall, and he grabbed them and threw them on, then stepped out of the room.

As he stepped into the hall, all was quiet. Will assumed that most everyone would be sleeping in, as exhausted as they had all been. He knew he should be getting as much rest as possible since they had another treacherous day ahead, but the thought that he might get to kill David Ellis today, the man who had murdered his mother, weighed too heavy on his mind.

Will walked toward the break room, his lumbering gate almost like that of the Empties. As he got closer to the door, the fresh morning scent of roasted coffee hit his nostrils. He took a deep breath to take it in and he could feel at least a little bit of his stress fade away. *Somebody must already be awake.*

When he walked through the doorway, Will saw Jessica sitting alone at the end of the table. A steaming mug sat on the table, cupped between her hands. She glanced up at him, and her eyes appeared heavy. Her hair was slightly a mess.

"Couldn't sleep either?" she asked.

Will narrowed his eyes. "How could you tell?"

She smiled. "Sit down. I'll pour you a cup of coffee."

Will grabbed an open chair on the long side of the table near Jessica and sat down. Behind him, he listened to coffee mugs clank together in the cabinet and then he heard the sweet sound of the liquid gold flowing into the cup. She set it down in front of him, along with some cream and sugar.

"Thanks," Will said, looking at her and smiling as she sat back down. Her smile back told him he was welcome, and she took another sip of her coffee.

"You get any sleep at all?" Will asked.

Jessica shook her head. "I'm pretty sure for half the night I wasn't even in bed. I spent a lot of time at the window, just looking outside." There was a brief silence, then Jessica continued. "You think things will ever go back to how they were?"

Will shook his head. "I don't know."

"I should be in my car right now, listening to an audiobook and on my way to work," Jessica explained. "It's amazing how much you miss routine and normalcy when it's all just taken from you."

Will thought back to his old day job. Even though it had been a shit, labor-intensive gig, he did miss it. He missed being around all the guys and, like Jessica had said, the routine.

"Well, I have to think that someone is out there trying to find a cure for whatever this thing is," Will said.

"If it is something that can be cured at all," Jessica added.

Will let the thought sit in the air for a moment. He sipped his coffee, trying to gather a reply, but decided to change the subject.

"So, you definitely heard those directions to this farm correctly?"

Jessica nodded. "One hundred percent sure."

"Good."

"Have you guys figured out what the plan is yet?" Jessica asked.

Will shook his head. "Supposed to meet with Gabriel and Marcus this morning to try and figure things out. Losing Brandon and Sam is a big blow."

Jessica looked at Will. "You can't blame yourself for what they did.".

"It's hard not to," Will said. "I should have just dragged Brandon out of that house."

"You said yourself, he threatened to shoot you. And Sam

had been bit. You can't fault his decision."

"I don't think he actually would've shot me," Will said. He bowed his head. "He was just wasting too much fucking time. I was scared that something would happen to you, and I wanted to get out of that house and get you the hell out of there."

When he glanced back up at Jessica, she looked down to avoid his gaze. He could see the red in her cheeks.

"You know, I meant what I said last night," Jessica said. "I understand why he did what he did. He made the only choice he felt was right. He quit. Plain and simple. On the world, on us, but more than anything, on himself." She looked up now and stared blankly into a wall. "When I saw my parents lying on that bed, I crumbled. I felt like my entire world was lost. Like nothing mattered anymore. I was ready to let go and to quit, but your mom saved me. Difference is, I really wanted to live, and she was there to show me that. Brandon didn't."

She looked back to Will and he barely held back from crying, the thought of his dead mother still so close. Eventually, he knew his guilt over Brandon's death would subside, but he was so stressed that it was easy to carry that burden on his back for now. But what Jessica had said helped ease some of the pain.

Footsteps crept in from outside and Will quickly dabbed at his eyes. He turned to see Marcus.

"Morning," Marcus said.

"Good morning," Jessica replied. Will waved.

Marcus looked to Will. "You 'bout ready? I can go grab Gabriel."

"Yeah," Will said. "I'll meet you down at his room and we can talk in there."

"Alright," Marcus replied. "Might wanna bring him some coffee, though."

"Will do."

As Marcus left the room, Will looked over to Jessica.

"Thank you, again."

She waved. "Don't mention it."

"It's gonna be a long day," Will said. "Might want to try and go get some sleep."

"I'll think about it."

***

Gabriel

When Will and Marcus came knocking on the door, Gabriel had already been awake for almost a half hour. Knowing how exhausting the day ahead would be, he'd decided to stay in bed for as long as he could. For all he knew, it might be the last chance he ever got to sleep in a real bed.

"Come in," Gabriel said, and Will and Marcus entered the room, the latter shutting the door behind them.

Gabriel immediately noticed the redness of Will's eyes, the bags under them, and how he almost looked as pale and soulless as one of the Empties.

"You get you some sleep?" Gabriel asked Will.

"Doesn't matter," Will replied.

Doesn't matter? Gabriel thought. *We're about to start a fucking war and it doesn't matter that you look like you can barely hold your head up?* He wanted to say these things out loud, but decided against it. Better not to start a different kind of war right here before they headed out to find Dylan.

"Brought you some coffee," Will said, offering Gabriel a mug.

"Thought I smelled that." He took the cup. "Thanks."

"So," Marcus began, "we need to come up with a game plan for how all this is gonna go down today."

"Pretty simple if you ask me," Will said. "We drive there and we find Dylan and David. And whatever or whoever gets in our way, we take 'em down."

Gabriel chuckled. "That's your plan, Rambo?"

Will nodded conclusively. "Yeah, it is."

"We have no idea what we're going into here," Marcus said. "We don't know anything about this farm; not how many people are there, what kind of firearms they are packing, or how they have it secured. Hell, we could be walking right into a trap."

"Assuming David went back and lied to them, and told them that we killed those two rednecks, they're gonna either be waiting on us or they're gonna show up here at some point. Now, I agree, we need to go to them before they get to us, but we can't just go in there with guns blazing."

"Well, you got a better plan?" Will asked.

Gabriel smiled. "Yeah, actually, I do."

CHAPTER TWELVE

<u>Dylan</u>

The light shone in through the room and Dylan awoke to find he was still alone. It was a miracle he'd been able to sleep at all; absolute exhaustion had to be the only reason he'd been able to. He looked to the door and saw that something wrapped in white paper had been slipped under it. He jumped up and hurried over.

Written on top of the piece of paper that covered the object was the word "Breakfast". Dylan frowned once he read the note, and opened it up to reveal an off-brand granola bar. His stomach howled at the sight of it and tears filled his eyes. The boy let go of the bar, wrestled himself to his feet, and started to bang on the door.

"Let me out of here! Please, let me out!"

The floors creaked and heavy footsteps marched down the hall. Dylan stopped beating on the door and backed away.

It violently swung open, the knob slamming against the wall, and the large dirty man's shadow eclipsed Dylan. The man walked toward him, the wrapper of the granola bar crinkling as it was crushed under his huge boot. Dylan shuddered, backing up until he hit the mattress.

"I'm sorry," Dylan said. "I'm sorry I yelled and banged on the door. I promise I'll be quiet. Just, please, don't hurt me."

But the man was already leaning down and reaching for Dylan. The boy yelled, but the large man ignored him and picked him up, throwing the child over his shoulder like a sand bag.

Dylan bounced up and down, his head hanging halfway down the man's broad backside. This was only the second time he'd been outside of the room since they'd brought him into the house, and he was finally able to get a good look at the place. He was being carried down a long hallway and, so far, they'd passed three other rooms. The floors were old and unfinished, appearing to be simple 2x4s like he had used when he'd helped his dad build a fence around their backyard. Pictures hung on the walls, but the man was moving too fast for Dylan to get a good look at them.

The stairs crackled as the man stepped down them, and Dylan's yelling had turned into heavy breathing. Where was the man taking him?

When they reached the lower level of the house, Dylan saw a sofa that looked twice as old as he was sitting in front of a beat-up television. Two teenage girls wearing identical dresses sat on the couch, their eyes glued to one of those boring morning talk shows, barely visible through the static.

If Dylan's stomach hadn't been empty, he would've probably thrown up when he was tossed off of the man's shoulder and set down into a chair. He was placed in front of a large wooden table, and two familiar faces sat at the other end of it. Clint sat at the very end of the table, a large plate of meat and eggs in front of him, and Cindy sat to his immediate left. Two children sat in chairs on either side of Dylan, each looking like they hadn't ever traveled more than a few miles from the farm. Both of them were boys, neither wearing a shirt, and their faces stained with dirt. One of the boys, who may have just been a year or two shy of Dylan's age, smiled at him, revealing the absence of most of his teeth.

A few moments after he settled, his veins redistributing the blood from his head to the rest of his body, the smell hit him. The stench of sour milk mixed with steak and eggs. He could also smell the two boys. It all congealed in the air to form a rotten odor that almost made Dylan puke even though his belly was empty.

The shadow of the large man appeared over Dylan, and he slapped a plate down in front of the boy. Runny eggs mixed together with some other food Dylan was pretty sure he'd never seen before. It looked gross enough to almost make him want to ask for another expired shake or granola bar.

"Go ahead, son," Clint said. "Eat."

Dylan stared at the slop for another minute, then looked up at Clint with weak eyes, on the verge of bursting.

"Can I take this back up to my room?" Dylan asked.

Clint's eyes narrowed, and Dylan immediately regretted the question. The shadow reached down to steal the plate from him, and then he walked it back toward the kitchen.

"No!" Dylan cried out. "Please, I'm sorry. I'll eat here; just please bring my plate back. I didn't mean to offend anybody."

The large man turned to Clint, and Clint nodded at him to return the platter to the table. He set the plate back down in front of Dylan, then picked up the fork and put it in the boy's hand. The large man retreated again, and Clint and Cindy continued to eat their food at the other end of the table. The two boys just stared at Dylan, ignoring their food and apparently waiting to see what his next move would be.

Dylan stirred the white-ish substance on the plate, then looked up to Clint and asked, "What is this?"

Peeking over the salt and pepper shakers at the center of the table, Clint looked at the plate and chuckled. "In America, we call that eggs and grits."

"What are grits?" Dylan asked, scrunching up his face.

"Where you from, boy?" Clint asked.

"Alexandria," Dylan mumbled, slightly embarrassed that he didn't know what grits were.

"Where's that?"

"In Virginia. Right outside of Washington D.C."

"Fuckin' hippies," Clint said. "Just eat it, kid."

Dylan looked up, and the smelly boys still stared at him. He tried to put them out of his mind, and pretend like the plate in front of him was full of his mother's delicious, fluffy eggs. Just as he realized how dry his throat was, the large man came back over and set down a glass of water in front of him. It had a slightly brown tint to it, but he wasn't going to complain. He'd likely rather have that over the sour milk, and he knew he would need something to wash the slop down with.

Without thinking about it, Dylan forced the first bite into his mouth, trailing the mush with a large swig of the dirty water. He could taste the minerals in the water mixing with the nasty taste of the egg and grits mixture, and covered his mouth so he could swallow without throwing up. If he didn't eat what they'd offered, there was no telling when or if the people would feed him again. He had no choice but to force it down.

One of the children giggled, and Cindy hit him across the back of his head with an open palm. The child's head snapped down, almost slamming his nose into the table.

"You shut the fuck up and eat your food," she shouted.

The boy rubbed the back of his head and glared at Dylan as if it was his fault he'd been slapped.

Clint looked over to Dylan, who was trying to swallow his second bite of breakfast. "We gonna let you spend some time with us today. Show you the real fun stuff."

Dylan nearly threw up, barely hearing Clint speak as he was trying to make himself swallow another disgusting bite. Clint took another bloody bite out of his steak.

"Yeah, you gonna have fun with us today, boy. That, I promise."

The stairs creaked as heavy footsteps moved downward. Dylan looked up and his eyes widened as he saw a smiling familiar face. An uneasy feeling crept up inside him. Clint smiled.

"Perfect timing," Clint said. "We were just finishing up breakfast before we go and get started for the day." Clint looked to Dylan and pointed at the man. "Dylan, I'm not sure you've been properly introduced. This is Mr. David Ellis."

CHAPTER THIRTEEN

<u>Jessica</u>

Writing had always been Jessica's number one way of relaxation and escape, and now she was thankful she'd mentioned her love of the craft to Sarah in passing during a conversation that morning. When she'd gone back to her room after breakfast, there lay a blank notepad and a pen waiting for her on her bed, along with a simple note that just had a smiley face drawn on it.

She'd spent the past hour lying on the bed on her stomach, writing in her new journal. It brought her a certain calm to finally get the words out onto the page. She wasn't the kind who was typically comforted by speaking her emotions out loud with other people and trying to sort through them. She found writing them down to be a much better therapy.

Jessica had just reached the part in her story where Walt pulled her into the hotel room, thus saving her, when a knock came at the door.

"Come in," she said.

The door opened and Holly poked her head through. "Will, Gabriel, and Marcus want to talk to everyone. They're asking everyone to meet out at the nurses' station in about twenty minutes."

Jessica nodded. "Cool, thanks."

She'd looked back down to continue writing when she saw Holly enter the room out of the corner of her eye. Jessica shut the notebook and looked up to Holly again. Her arms crossed, Holly glared at Jessica.

"Yes?" Jessica asked.

"I love him."

Jessica was at a loss for words. How was she supposed to respond to that?

"I know that you guys are getting close," Holly continued. "You've got a special connection to him because of his mother, I get that. But just don't get too close."

With that last sentence, Jessica went from feeling slightly awkward to a little bit angry.

"Are you threatening me?"

"Not yet," Holly said, shaking her head. She turned and opened the door, glaring back at Jessica one more time before she left the room.

Staring down at her notebook, Jessica shook her head. She hopped off the bed and headed to the restroom for a quick shower, being sure to take her notebook with her so she could keep it close.

***

When Jessica left her room and headed to the nurses' station, the rest of the group was already standing there. She made a point of looking for Sarah first, whose eyes went to the journal under Jessica's arm, and she smiled. Jessica smiled back and mouthed the words "Thank you."

"Nice of you to join us," Holly said in a snarky tone.

Jessica took one look at Holly and then looked away. The girl was obviously trying to intimidate her, but the schoolyard antics weren't going to do anything to impress her.

Will either didn't notice her snobbish tone or didn't care. He looked focused on more important things as he began to speak.

"Thanks everyone for meeting here. Before I get started, I just want to take a moment to thank everyone for their support over the last day. It's been the hardest couple of days of my life, and I thank you. I know it wasn't made any easier last night when we lost three more people, but everyone has remained strong." He stopped for a moment to clear his throat and gather his thoughts.

"Everyone here knows that one of our own was taken by some redneck savages. A young, helpless boy. And it's no secret that the man who killed my mother and Kristen, and who was responsible for the death of Trevor, is more than likely there with them." He had to stop again. Jessica could see in his face that the utter thought of David Ellis jolted Will's nerves. Gabriel leaned over to whisper something into Will's ear, but Will shook his head and then continued. "Gabriel, Marcus, and myself have come up with a plan to rescue the boy. We're here today so we can get your opinion. This is going to require everyone to contribute, and it's going to be dangerous."

Jessica looked to Holly again, who was staring up at Will. The girl was scared, no doubt. Much more scared than Jessica. Jessica was prepared to do what she needed to do to help the group move forward, whatever the cost might be.

"So," Will said. "Here's what we're gonna do."

***

Jessica was the first one to walk away when Will and Gabriel were through talking and everyone had agreed on the plan. She headed to her room, but she immediately heard approaching footsteps and turned around to see Will.

"Are you okay?" Will asked.

"Yeah, I'm fine," Jessica nodded.

Will shook his head. "You don't have to do this."

"It's okay," Jessica said. "I want to do it. Really. It can't be you, Holly, or Marcus. And Sarah is way too scared. So, that just leaves me."

His hand landed on her arm and his face moved closer to hers. "We're gonna be right behind you. I promise. I won't let anything happen to you." Will leaned in and hugged her, and as she looked back down the hall over his shoulder, Jessica saw Holly glaring at her.

Will pulled away. "Go get some rest. We're gonna head out in just a couple of hours."

CHAPTER FOURTEEN

Dylan

As soon as he finished eating his steak and egg breakfast, Clint slammed his hands on the table and jumped to his feet. It startled Dylan, who almost choked as he was trying to force down more of his slop. He looked up to see the large man looking down to Clint and nodding.

"Everything's ready?" Clint asked.

The oversized man nodded. A grin stretched across Clint's face.

Cindy stood and looked down at the two boys sitting next to Dylan.

"Go to your room!" she demanded.

The two boys promptly stood up and dashed up the stairs, refraining from speaking, though one of them giggled.

The woman stomped over to Dylan and grabbed him by the arm, pinching the skin around his bicep. The boy cried out, but she ignored him and dragged him away anyway.

"Where are you taking me?" Dylan asked.

"Shut up," Cindy said.

Clint and David walked a few paces in front of them, talking to each other. Dylan wasn't able to make out what they were saying, and he was too focused on the pain in his arm for it to matter.

When they stepped outside, he immediately put his free

hand over his eyes. It had been a couple of days since he'd been out in the sun, and in that short amount of time, his eyes had already forgotten how bright it was. A gentle breeze carried an autumn chill in the air which brushed against the boy's skin through his clothes.

For the first time, he saw outside of the home he'd been a prisoner in. He looked across the large yard of overgrown grass to see the old barn that he assumed was the same one he'd spent time in when he'd first arrived there, before he'd been knocked out and dragged over to the house. From the outside, the barn looked like it could crumble at any given moment. Mismatched colored boards patched holes in the structure, and tall discolored grass surrounded it.

Dylan's attention returned to where the people were leading him. A table sat in a part of the yard where the unkempt grass became dirt. An old, full-grown tree shaded the area. When the group moved close enough to the table for Dylan to see what lay on top of it, his eyes widened.

A woman, appearing to be in her early twenties, lay in the middle of the table. He hadn't gotten a good enough look at the girl's in the barn to know if she was one of two that had been in the barn with him. Her hands and feet were bound to the table and her mouth was gagged. Her muffled screaming sent a chill through Dylan, and as they got closer to her, she looked over at the group and her eyes met Dylan's. The young boy didn't know a person's eyes could be so red. There was a pain in them that he would not be able to understand until later in his life. He might, in fact, never understand it. But what he did understand was the fear inside him as he looked at the girl.

"Go ahead, Horace," Clint said, looking to the large man.

Dylan looked to where Horace was walking and he noticed a small shack about twenty-five yards away from where they stood, just outside the looming shadow of the old tree. He noticed that the door on the metal building was moving.

The boy's attention turned away from the shack when he heard a commotion coming from the barn. He looked over and saw the doors open. Two men appeared from the inside. One of them was a man with long, stringy hair, wearing a sleeveless plaid shirt that was unbuttoned to reveal his bare chest underneath. He was holding another man by the shirt and Dylan recognized the man instantly.

It was the preacher.

The long-haired man brought the preacher over near the table, then shoved him, causing the priest to fall down into the dirt.

"Please, don't make me do this again," the preacher cried.

Clint knelt down next to the preacher, and for the first time, Dylan noticed the holster around his waist, housing a handgun.

"Samuel, Samuel, Samuel," Clint said to the preacher. "This is God's work now. Isn't that what you're all about?"

The preacher breathed heavy. "But I am not Him, Brother Clint. I cannot do what you ask. I am but a mortal man."

Clint laughed. "Yeah, well, we'll see about that. Surely, you won't let another one die."

Samuel crumbled to the ground and clasped the dirt.

"I'm anxious to see this," David said.

Clint patted him on the back. "Well, then, let's get the

party started." He looked over to Horace and the long-haired man, who'd joined Horace by the shed.

Horace held a long pole with a hoop at the end. He nodded to the long-haired man, who nodded back and then opened the door to the shed.

A boy, a teenager probably no more than five years Dylan's senior, walked out of the shed. But he was no longer just a teenager. His skin looked old and battered, blood stains circling his mouth, and his eyes were pale. The boy was Empty.

The girl on the table didn't even have to look back to see what they'd pulled from the shed. She screamed.

The Empty lumbered toward Horace, but the skinny long-haired man waved his arms and whistled.

"Hey, come on over here," the man called. "Come to Danny." The Empty turned from Horace and walked toward Danny. "Come 'ere, you dumb piece-a-shit."

Danny backed up as Horace brought up the pole and then wrapped the hoop at the end of it around the creature's neck. Once Horace had him secure, Danny moved to where his back faced the group, and he started to walk backward toward the table. The Empty followed, reaching out its arms, ignoring the noose around its neck.

Dylan looked up to Clint and David. Both men had their arms crossed, smiles across their faces.

"What are you doing?" Dylan asked.

Neither man looked down, but Dylan felt a pop on the back of his head and cried out, reaching back to rub his skull.

"Shut the fuck up," Cindy commanded him. He looked up to the woman, tears now filling his eyes, and she glared down at him.

Dylan turned his attention to the preacher, Samuel, who was down on all fours, his face in the dirt, mumbling a prayer to himself. The girl on the table had tears pouring down the sides of her face as she continued to try and break free from the restraints. All the while, Danny was approaching the table, still taunting the beast.

Danny moved to where his back was against the side of the table. The Empty was only a few feet away from him, reaching his arms out and trying to grab the hillbilly.

"I hope you're ready, Preacher," Danny said, not letting his eyes leave the Empty.

"Please, don't do this," Samuel said, looking up for a moment as he gripped a cross on his chest.

"Now!" Danny shouted.

On Danny's command, Horace slacked up on the beast, sure to still keep hold of him, and the Empty lunged toward Danny. The long-haired man dove out of the way, but the creature continued its snarling lunge. But instead of biting Danny, it dug its teeth into the girl's arm.

The grotesque sound of the initial bite buried itself into Dylan's ears. It was like watching a car crash. When he'd been seven years old, Dylan had witnessed a head-on collision, and remembered not being able to look away. Watching the Empty sink its teeth into the helpless girl's arm as she squirmed, almost as if she were having a seizure, was a similar experience. Dylan couldn't turn his head. He was in shock.

What was more sickening than the feast in front of him was that the two men, David and Clint, continued to stand with their arms crossed, grinning. Dylan's young mind couldn't process how the two men could be getting so much enjoyment out of seeing the girl suffer. He'd never seen this level of hatred.

"That's good," Clint said, holding his hand up to Horace as if to tell him to stop, and Horace pulled the Empty away from the girl.

Danny ran around the table and taunted the creature again; once more, it followed him back toward the shed.

Dylan caught a glimpse of the girl's bite mark. Blood drained from the round wound which was slowly fading to black. The distaste hung in Dylan's throat from the disgusting breakfast, and he turned and threw the slop up all over the dirt. It looked just as nasty coming back out of him as it had going in.

Clint went to Samuel and grabbed him by the collar. He forced Samuel to his feet and dragged him over to the girl's side, where the wound was. The young girl had given up trying to break loose, and now just cried, her body bouncing.

"Alright, Brother Samuel. Are you really willing to let this girl die?" Clint asked.

"Please," Samuel cried. "God be with this young girl, for I am mortal, and I cannot help her."

Clint grabbed a handful of Samuel's salt and pepper hair and yanked his head back. Anger filled his raised voice. "Is that it, Preacher? Are you just gonna let this bitch die? Are you?"

Dylan could see the girl looking at Samuel, as if begging him to save her.

Samuel's eyes went to Clint's. "I cannot—"

"Save her!" Clint moved the preacher's head back to the wound. "Pull the demon out of her! You're running out of time!"

Dylan saw the preacher shudder and close his eyes as he started to pray.

"Dear Heavenly Father, it is with heavy hearts we come to you. You are full of grace, Almighty Creator. Our hearts are heavy because of this life that is leaving us. Death engulfs us, Lord..."

Dylan had heard this prayer before. Pastor Dennis, the preacher at his church back home in Virginia, had said this same prayer to one of Dylan's cousins, just before she'd died of cancer. Clint's eyes narrowed. He'd apparently heard this before, too, and it wasn't what he'd expected Samuel to say.

"Ah, fuck!" Clint yelled. He pulled Samuel down by the back of his shirt and then drew his gun, directing it at the preacher's head. Dylan gasped as the pistol clicked, sending a round into the chamber.

"Wait," David said, breaking his silence.

With the gun still pointed at the preacher, ready to end his life at any moment Clint chose, Clint looked to David.

"Don't kill him. Not yet," David said. He looked down at the girl. "Maybe if you bring him out here later to see what he's done, he won't let it happen again."

In the distance, the door to the shed closed, as Horace and Danny had led the beast back inside. Danny reached up to give Horace a high-five, though he ignored him, and they made their way back toward the group.

Clint looked back down at Samuel, contemplating what David had suggested. The preacher mumbled a new prayer to himself, now begging that God would guide him into Heaven, as he would be joining Him soon. Clint lowered the gun, then looked back at Horace and Danny.

"Get this piece of shit to his feet and back to the barn," he commanded them. "And leave her there. Mr. Ellis is right. Maybe if he sees her become a demon, he won't let it happen again."

"Help me!" the girl cried. Dylan could just make out the muffled words.

Tears ran down the girl's face, and Dylan wanted so badly to go to her and at least cover her arm. Bugs had already begun to surround it. He wanted to press the wound so it could stop bleeding. She looked to him one more time, her eyes even redder than before, and he finally had to turn away.

"Come on," Cindy said, and she grabbed Dylan's arm again and turned him around.

The dying girl mumbled, and the preacher cried out as the toothless woman led Dylan back to the house.

CHAPTER FIFTEEN

David

After the failed experiment with the preacher and the young girl, Clint led David back into the house. Cindy followed, guiding the kidnapped boy back up the stairs. David took one glance at the child, then continued to follow Clint into a room on the other side of the kitchen.

"Come on in," Clint told David, holding a door open for him.

David walked inside the small space and took a seat in a chair against the wall. An unmade bed sat against the wall next to him, the sheets looking like they hadn't been changed in a long time. They carried a musty smell with them as proof. A few beer cans had been tossed on the floor near a trash can, but not in it. Against the opposite wall sat a desk. On top of it, an old CB radio. Clint took a seat in the chair in front of the desk. He pulled out a cigarette and lit it, offering one to David, who declined. He was disgusted that the man smoked in the house, especially in such a small room. But not wanting to stir any nerves, he kept the matter to himself.

Clint pointed toward the door with his cigarette in hand and asked, "You think they'll come looking for that boy?"

David nodded. "Not sure they'll have a shot in hell of actually finding us, but yeah, I think they could try. I still don't understand why you don't just wanna go to the hospital and get them. They'll be like sitting ducks. We have all their weapons."

Clint laughed. "Trust me, bud, I do. But this here shit with the preacher is important. I think he has answers. Besides, let them sweat it out a little bit at the hospital. They have to know we'll come for 'em eventually since they killed two of our people."

On the inside, David smiled, but he didn't show it on his face. He still had the redneck thinking that the two men he'd shot, Trent and Cody, had actually been killed by someone in Will's group. Truth be told, it had felt good to kill the two men.

Clint narrowed his eyes and pointed his cigarette toward David, the smoke floating toward him.

"You said, the nigger who shot Trent and Cody, his name was Marcus?"

David nodded.

"Well, when we do finally go pay that hospital a visit, I'm gonna hang that spook right in front of everyone before I put a bullet in each of 'em."

"As long as you give me Will, I'll be satisfied." A smile formed in David's mind about the fact that he would finally be ready to kill Will the next time he saw him. That he would be broken, and suffer.

Clint smiled. "Ya know, I'm glad I didn't shoot you when I found you hanging with that stupid darky that we killed. You're all right, Mr. Ellis."

"Tell me then," David said. "What is it with the preacher?"

Clint's cigarette was almost down to the filter, and he

smashed it into an ash tray on the table. He clasped his hands, his elbows on his knees, and looked at David.

"I think he knows how to reverse what's going on with those monsters."

David furrowed his brow. "Really? How do you figure?"

"'Cause I think they're demons and that he has the power to exorcise them."

After taking a moment to stare at Clint to see if he was joking, David laughed when he realized the man was being serious. "What the fuck is so funny?" Clint asked.

Getting his laughter to calm, David said, "I'm sorry to be the one to tell you, but demons aren't real. You've got a better chance of bangin' Kate Upton than you do of seeing some little red guy come up out of that girl out there."

"It ain't gonna be like that," Clint replied. "That's not how they look. In fact, I doubt we'd ever even see them, but they're there."

In his mind, David continued to laugh. The fact that the redneck actually thought all these people had been possessed by demons, as opposed to infected with something viral, was silly. A fairytale.

"Okay, so let's say these things *are* possessed. Where did you even get that idea in the first place, and what do you think that preacher can do to 'heal' them? Because, let me tell you, there's nothing in Revelation that says Lucifer will turn half the human race into flesh-eating monsters to roam the earth and hunt the last of us. That's silly.""

"The Bible has been passed down for thousands of years, and there are many lost books. Many believe that one of the lost books of the New Testament had a different translation of the apocalypse than the one we've come to know from Revelation. One that says demons will infect the world and spread out amongst the living until the human race is vanished, and all that remains are the spirits of the Dark Lord. I know it's hard to believe, Mr. Ellis. I've been going to church my whole life, a proud Southern Baptist, and this shit seems just as out there to me as it does to you. But I think it's real. And I think Samuel can prove it."

"Well, he sure didn't prove shit out there other than the fact he knows how to pray," David said. "And if he does indeed know how to 'cure' everyone, he's sure willing to let an innocent girl die to hide it. And let's pretend for a moment that all this is real... what makes you think he can stop it?"

"Trent, one of the men who took you to the hospital, in case you don't remember, has known Samuel for a long time. Not friends, but the preacher grew up with Trent's wife. Trent said that the preacher has been talking about this shit for years. He even overheard him a few days before all this shit happened. Samuel was down the street at the truck stop goin' on and on about the end of the world and the 'demons'. So, when all this stuff happened, one of the first things we did was go find Samuel."

Clint smiled. "In time, David. You'll see. We have plenty more sacrifices in line. Eventually, his guilt will get to him, and he will at least *try* to perform an exorcism."

"And what if it doesn't work?"

Clint shrugged. "Then I guess we won't need the preacher anymore." He looked down at his watch. "In thirty minutes, we'll go get him. The bitch should be turned by then. We'll see how he feels once he sees what he's done."

***

Dylan

The door swung open and Cindy almost literally tossed Dylan into his room. He was small, but he was still surprised by the woman's strength, her being able to nearly throw a squirming eleven year old boy.

As he lay on his stomach, gripping the carpet, the door slammed behind him and he heard the deadbolt turn into the lock from the outside. Cindy's feet stomped across the floor, but then his ears turned to something else. It was a noise inside the room. Shuddering and heavy breathing. Dylan got up onto his knees and looked over to the wall, and his eyes widened.

"Mary Beth."

The girl was curled up in the corner of the room on her bed. Dylan rose to his feet and hurried over to her. When he got closer, he could see that she was shaking, almost as if she were cold. He moved onto the center of the bed on his knees and reached out toward her.

"Mary Beth, are you—"

"Don't touch me!"

Dylan jumped back. Her tone was sharp and demanding. It threw him off-guard. He moved to the edge of the bed, clasping his hands together.

"M-Mary Beth, what's wrong?"

"They're going to kill me."

Dylan narrowed his eyes. "What do you mean? Who's going to kill you?"

"Them," Mary Beth replied. She was nearly inarticulate

through her crying. "The bad people downstairs."

"What? Why do you think they're gonna kill you?"

"They're gonna turn me into one of *them*."

"Them what?" Dylan didn't understand.

A gunshot rang from outside, startling both of the children. Dylan looked over toward the window, then back down at Mary Beth. She was now pointing at the window.

"One of them."

Dylan hopped off the bed and hurried over to the window.

A man in a hat with long hair pumped a shotgun. Dylan recognized him as Danny as he hollered, and then he aimed the gun in front of him. The branches of a tree hid what he was aiming at. Another shot went off, and Dylan saw a body fall out from the shadow of the trees. It was an Empty. Dylan looked back over toward Mary Beth.

"You think they're gonna turn you into an Empty?"

Mary Beth finally looked up from hugging herself. "A what?"

"Sorry. That's what we called those monsters in the group I was with before. Empties."

"Oh," she replied, wiping tears from her eyes. "Those two little boys who are here in the house, they told me that the bad people were going to take me out there and turn me into one of those things. They said something about a table and how they have one of the creatures—an Empty, you called it —locked up."

Dylan had to look away from the girl. He thought about everything he'd just witnessed outside and knew he wouldn't be able to keep what he'd seen to himself if she started asking questions. He'd never been one to successfully keep a secret. Any time one of his friends or classmates told him a secret, the kid wouldn't even have to have their back turned before Dylan was already telling someone else. But in this case, he didn't want the girl to be anymore frightened than she already was.

"I don't want them to bite me, Dylan. I don't want them to hurt me."

Dylan went back to the bed. He thought back to when Holly had been upset and how Will had wrapped his arm around her to try and comfort her. *Worth a shot.*

The young boy reluctantly put his arm around the frightened girl, and she nestled into his chest. It was strange. He'd never held a girl before who wasn't his mom.

"Please, Dylan. Don't let them hurt me."

"I won't."

Now Dylan just had to figure out how he could keep that promise if someone did come to grab her.

CHAPTER SIXTEEN

David

For the past twenty minutes, David had been flipping through the Book of Revelation in a New King James Bible that he'd found in the drawer of the table next to his bed. Even though Clint had claimed that it was a lost book that prophesied demons would come to Earth and possess the human race, he scanned each verse, looking for any kind of hint that any of this could be true. Even if that proclamation was in a lost book, he thought there might still be a chance that some of the story could be tied into Revelation. After a time searching the text for clues, he closed the book and put it down.

"This is bullshit."

A knock came at the door.

"Come in."

The large burly man known as Horace stepped into the doorway. Under the bright light in the room, the man was even uglier than David had thought, as he hadn't really looked at him carefully until now. Horace nodded his head toward the front door.

"He's going out there now?" David asked, speaking of Clint.

Horace nodded.

Opening the drawer of the side table, David shoved the

Bible back inside. *I'll come back to these fairytales later.*

***

Clouds moved in, creating an overcast sky above the farm. Blocking the sun, they also made the already nice Fall day a little bit cooler. Clint greeted David on the spacious front porch and threw him a long-sleeve plaid shirt.

"Here ya go, partner."

"Thanks," David said. The shirt reeked of tobacco, but he put it on anyway to keep warm.

The front patio stretched the length of the long house and had a floor made of old, wooden slats. A row of what looked to be homemade rocking chairs lined the porch, and two of them squeaked as the two young, shirtless boys rocked back and forth in them. They both stared at David, stoic expressions masking their faces. A hand clasped onto David's shoulder and he turned.

"Come on," Clint said. "Let's go check on that bitch." He pointed sternly at the two boys. "You two pricks stay right here and keep your mouths shut, you hear me?"

"Yes, Pop," one of the boys said.

David and Clint headed down the porch steps and started toward the table under the tree. David turned his head when he saw Danny racing up the driveway toward them.

"Woo, I killed me four of those bastards!" Danny said.

"Have you been over here to check on the girl yet?" Clint asked.

"Shit nah, man. Been havin' me too much fun."

Clint shook his head and then looked back at David. "See the kinda shit I gotta put up with?"

"What?" Danny said, his arms out quizzically.

122

"Just take your dumb ass over to the barn. I think we're gonna have a live one here and I'm gonna signal you when I want you to let the preacher out."

Danny scoffed. "Yes, sir." He slung the shotgun over his shoulder and headed for the barn.

The sun peeked out from one of the clouds, and David used his hand as a visor to look toward the table where they'd left the girl. She still squirmed, just like when they had left her there, but even over his footsteps through the tall grass, he could hear the snarls.

The girl on the table was Empty.

The gag had been removed so that Samuel could hear the girl scream as she died, and her mouth was agape as she hissed and tried to break free from the straps holding her down. Ten yards away from the table, David could see the veins protruding from her now pale skin, and she looked to him with inhuman eyes. Clint patted David on the back, a smile covering his face.

"Woohoo, boys! We got us a live one!"

After he yelled, the resident biter inside the shack started to bang against the metal structure. Clint waved toward Danny, who stood in front of the barn.

"Go on, Danny-boy! Bring that bastard out here to see what he done! I bet he can't wait to hear her scream!"

Danny gave Clint a thumbs up, then swung the large barn door open. When he re-appeared a couple of minutes later, he tossed Samuel onto the ground in front of him, pointing the shotgun at the preacher and demanding that he stand. Samuel stumbled to his feet and walked with his hands in the air, just like a prisoner of war.

Once the preacher walked far enough to where he could see the thing wrestling on the table, he crumbled to the ground.

"Get that piece of trash on his fuckin' feet," Clint demanded.

Danny reared his foot back and kicked Samuel square in his backside. The preacher hit the dirt face-first and coughed. Danny pumped the shotgun and pointed it down at the preacher's lower body.

"Get the fuck up or I'm gonna blow one of them chicken legs right off!"

"I want you to get your ass over here and see what you allowed to happen to this poor girl, Samuel," Clint said.

As Samuel rose to his feet, his eyes were closed and he prayed. Legs shaking, he walked toward the Empty lying on the table. Clint grabbed him and leaned him down toward it.

"Open your eyes, Samuel," Clint demanded.

The preacher continued to pray, his eyes remaining shut.

Clint reared his fist back and punched Samuel across his cheek. The preacher's eyes remained shut, and he never saw the punch coming. He fell onto the ground and grabbed at his face. Clint then reached down and took hold of the preacher by his collar, bringing him back to his feet. He led Samuel back over to the table and unsheathed a knife from his side.

"If you don't look down at her, I'll cut off your fucking eyelids so you don't have any other choice."

Tears dripped from the preacher's still closed eyes. David could see that Clint was losing his patience. Clint jerked the knife up toward Samuel's face, and the preacher finally gave in and opened his eyes.

The Empty glared at him with pale, bloodshot eyes. Samuel kept looking at it, just as Clint had asked, but his lips moved as he prayed for the creature. It snarled at him, spitting in his face. Samuel reached into his pocket and grabbed a handkerchief, wiping away the saliva dripping from his nose. Clint leaned down right next to the preacher's ear.

"You did this. This is your fault. You could have saved her, but you didn't. And why? To protect some ancient, holy secret?"

"Please, I don't know—"

"The hell you don't," Clint said, cutting him off. "I know you know how to do it. Just before all this happened, you were babblin' off at a truck stop and my friend Trent heard you. Said you were talkin' 'bout how only a 'pure soul could cure the wicked' and that you could do it."

The priest didn't respond. Clint scoffed.

"Well, we'll see if you can let another one die." Clint looked up to Danny. "Go tell Horace to come on."

***

Dylan

A light rain began to patter on the roof. The clinking of precipitation against the window drew young Dylan's attention away. He was still cuddled up with Mary Beth, working to soothe her. It'd worked, as the girl was now asleep against his chest. With the rain now coming down and clouds hiding the sun, Dylan found his own eyes beginning to get heavy, and he leaned the back of his head against the wall behind him.

His eyes weren't even shut for a minute before the deadbolt clicked over and the door was thrown open. Dylan opened his eyes wide, but Mary Beth didn't wake up until the door slammed against the wall behind it.

The large man they'd called Horace stood in the doorway, breathing heavy.

As he started toward the children, Mary Beth shuddered again. Dylan held her tight, hiding her face from the burly man.

"Stay away from her!" Dylan yelled.

Horace ignored him and reached down to grab the girl. Dylan punched at his arm. The look on Horace's face showed that he was surprised the boy was trying to fight back, but simply pushed Dylan aside and grabbed the girl. Mary Beth screamed.

In a last ditch effort to try and get the man away, Dylan leaned down and bit into his arm. Horace yelled out and stumbled back, clutching his arm, and Dylan saw his chance.

"Come on," he urged Mary Beth, and they stumbled off the bed and darted past Horace, out the door.

Dylan led Mary Beth, holding her hand. The hallway was vacant, and he saw a clear path to the front door.

Then, just as they were about to reach the stairs, Dylan tripped on something and went stumbling forward onto the wood floor. In the process, he dragged down Mary Beth, who cried out as she hit the ground just after him. When Dylan turned around to see what he'd tripped on, his eyes widened.

The two young boys who he'd seen at the table during breakfast stood over them. One of them held a hunting knife, the other a pistol. The kid with the hunting knife pointed it down at Dylan, smiling.

"Where you think you're going, squirt?" the kid asked.

Beyond the two boys, Horace came stammering out of the bedroom, still holding onto his arm where Dylan had bit him. He parted the two boys, pushing them against either wall, and grabbed Dylan, throwing him over his shoulder.

Still fighting, Dylan punched the man's broad backside, but it was no use.

When they reached the room, Horace drew Dylan off his shoulder and, without a care, flung the boy onto the floor from almost seven feet up. Dylan landed on his back on the wooden floor and winced. He flopped on the floor like a fish, never having felt this amount of pain before. The boy fought to catch his breath.

Dylan heard a slurping sound, and then he felt the man's spittle hit his cheek, only adding insult to injury. Horace slammed the door and set the deadbolt before he marched back down the hallway toward a weeping young girl. Crying more than he had since all this began, even more than he had from the plane crash, Dylan could only manage two words as he rolled around on the floor, wanting desperately for the sting in his back to disappear.

"Mary Beth!"

***

David

The oncoming storm didn't seem like it was going to faze Clint or put a stop to his torturous antics. The preacher continued to babble next to the Empty and Clint still laughed.

David turned when he heard the screen door open from

the front porch and heard the screams of a young girl.

"Now, here we go!" Clint hollered. He cupped his hands around his mouth and shouted, "Horace, bring that sweet thing over here!"

Whoever the girl was, Horace had her in one hand, and from where David stood, it looked like her feet might not have even been touching the ground. The closer she got, the more David was able to see how young she was. *Surely, he's not really going to kill a child.* That seemed a little much for even a man as cold as David Ellis.

"Danny," Clint said.

Danny looked and Clint just nodded.

The man must've understood what the leader of the group wanted, because he unsheathed a knife and walked to the side of the table. The creature looked up and hissed at him, and Danny stabbed it in the side of the head. The Empty lay still. Danny put the knife away and unstrapped the beast, rolling it off the table and onto the dirt below. Samuel continued to cry, praying for the thing that had once been a girl. Danny grabbed it by its legs and dragged it thirty yards off on the other side of a bush. David wondered if they had other bodies over there.

Behind him, the screams of the girl got louder as she and Horace approached. Danny arrived back from moving the creature's body, and wiped his hands with a towel before grabbing the new young girl's other arm. They held her in front of David, Samuel, and a smiling Clint.

"Well, hello, Miss Mary Beth," Clint said. "So nice of you to join us."

"Please, don't hurt me," Mary Beth said with a quake in

her voice.

"What are you doing, Clint?" David asked.

Clint smiled. "Just wait and see."

David clinched his fists. It was one thing to witness what had happened with the woman on the table earlier, but a child? The abuse brought back memories of his childhood and his alcoholic father.

Clint clicked his tongue and shrugged. "Unfortunately, that's not up to me, darlin'." He put his hand on Samuel's shoulder. "The good ole preacher here is gonna have to decide if he wants to keep playin' games and let you die, or if he is gonna quit bullshittin' and show us that he has the answer."

"The answer? What do you mean?" Mary Beth asked. "Please, just let me go!"

"I don't know what you want me to do!" Samuel cried. "Please, don't hurt this child."

Clint turned and pointed at the preacher. "Ya know, I'm running out of patience with you, Samuel," Clint said. He then looked over to Danny and Horace, and slapped his hand twice on the table.

The two men lifted the screaming girl up and lay her down on the table on her back. As might have been predicted, she screamed and fought them the entire time.

"Hold her down while I strap her in!" Danny said, looking at the mute man, Horace.

The oversized man only had to use a small amount of leverage to hold the young girl down. She still tried to fight loose, but it was pointless. Danny was easily able to secure her wrists with the leather straps, and then he repeated the same process with her ankles. Danny pulled a sock out of his pocket and went to stuff her mouth, but Clint grabbed his arm to stop him.

"Let her scream," Clint said. "I want Sammy-boy here to know she's in pain."

Samuel had his forehead pressed against the table next to Mary Beth's arms. David listened closely and could just barely hear the preacher mumbling the words, "I'm sorry."

Horace and Danny retreated to the tiny shack, and Mary Beth continued to plead for her life.

"Please, don't hurt me. Please, I'll do anything you want. Just don't hurt me."

Clint ignored her and she looked over to David.

"Mister, please help me. Don't let them do this to me!"

As was the routine, Horace grabbed the long pole, ready to capture the Empty when Danny let him out of the tiny shack. The structure rocked furiously, and David thought the beast might be more riled up than it had been before. Danny opened the door, and the beast stumbled out of the shack, snarling. Horace was able to quickly capture the Empty, and Danny began to taunt it.

Mary Beth screamed.

The young girl was inconsolable now, and Clint smiled like a child on Christmas morning. He reached down and grabbed Samuel by his hair, forcing him to watch the girl panic.

"Look at her, you piece of shit. You gonna let 'er die? Are you?"

"God, please look after this child, for You are almighty, Lord," Samuel said, ignoring Clint and continuing to pray.

"Yeah, well, we'll see just how mighty God is here in a few minutes."

Danny cussed at the creature, calling it 'ugly' and all kinds of other names. David's attention fell to the young girl again. Her eyes were puffy, and he saw so much desperation in them. He watched as she looked at him and mouthed the words, "Please, I don't wanna die." She didn't have a voice anymore.

It was finally more than even David could handle.

"I can't do this," David said, shaking his head. "I'm going inside."

Clint scoffed. "You fucking kidding me?"

But David just turned around and headed for the house, leaving the girl behind, screaming for him to help her. While he knew he'd already punched his ticket to Hell over the last few days with the things he'd done, even he wasn't cold enough to kill a child. He thought back to his teenage years and how his own father had abused him, his mother, and his little brother. There were a lot of things he could tolerate, but hurting a child wasn't one of them.

"Pussy!" Clint spat at him.

But David just continued to walk toward the house, his head down, trying to ignore the screaming girl behind him.

He reached the patio and the two boys were still in the rocking chairs, swaying back and forth and chewing on gum, or perhaps even tobacco, he thought, as backward as these people were. They stared at him through the posts in the guardrail, then he walked up the creaking steps. He tried to ignore them, but he could see them glaring at him from the corner of his eye.

Creepy fuckin' kids.

David took one last look out into the yard. Though he was a good distance away, the girl's screaming sounded as if it were almost right in front of him, its high shriek piercing through the cloudy sky. Danny was waving his arms, attracting the Empty ever so closer to the table. David turned back around, pushed open the door, and headed inside.

CHAPTER SEVENTEEN

<u>Jessica</u>

"You sure that's the place?" Gabriel asked.

Jessica turned to face him from the front seat. "I-I think so."

"That doesn't sound like such a sure answer," Holly sneered.

Jessica ignored her, and Will chimed in.

"We followed the directions. There's only one way to find out, I suppose."

Jessica took a deep breath and nodded as Will put his hand on her shoulder.

"You sure you wanna do this?" he asked.

"Yes," she said with confidence.

"We'll be right behind you. I promise."

Gabriel stepped out of the back seat, then coming to Jessica's door and opening it for her to get out. She thanked him and hugged him.

"You got this," Gabriel said. He jumped into the passenger seat.

Knowing they had to be close to the farmhouse where they'd find Dylan, they'd parked the truck off the side of the road. Jessica turned away from the truck and started walking away.

She wore a backpack over her good shoulder to make her

look more like a drifter. Even though she didn't really need it, she wore the sling on her injured arm. Will figured this might make her appear more innocent to strangers, and like someone who was in desperate need of help.

The ground sloped off the shoulder into a ditch, and the tall brush blocked the view of the land beyond. While she didn't know exactly which one of these houses was the one, she had a strange feeling she'd know it when she saw it.

Jessica passed the first driveway and looked through the break in the brush to see the remains of a home. It had been burned down and, by the looks of it, the accident had happened within the past week. Some of the white structure of the front of the house still stood, though most of the remains had been scarred black. Jessica turned back to the road and continued on.

Through a break in the brush, she was able to look into the vast front yard of the next home. She slowed down when she was sure she saw people outside. Jessica walked through the shallow ditch and kneeled down in front of the brush. She peeked through a gap and saw a few people gathered around a table. A large man held some kind of stick and moved like he was fighting something, but a small shack blocked most of her view. She looked back to the truck and gave the group a thumbs up, signaling she was pretty sure this was the place.

She made her way back onto the road and headed for the driveway. As she approached it, she saw the sign next to the mailbox that read "Hopkins Farm", confirming this was the place that the man had given direction to over the radio. The driveway was a curved dirt path leading up toward the house.

A large bush stood about halfway up, blocking her view of the front of the home, as well as the space where the people stood in the yard.

As she approached the bush, a foul smell hit her nostrils and she noticed flies buzzing around the tall grass that surrounded it. She covered her mouth and wretched, seeing a collection of rotted bodies under the large bush.

Once she passed this bush, she knew she'd be in full-view of the people standing outside. She closed her eyes, then stepped into the open.

When Jessica stepped around the corner, though, she couldn't believe what she saw.

She now had a clear view of what the large man with the pole was wrestling with. It was an Empty. Her mouth agape, her gaze focused on a table under a tree. A man stood beside it, while another kneeled next to it. On top of the table, a figure with long hair struggled. The person looked like they were bound to the table unwillingly.

What's going on here?

One of the men standing by the table looked over toward Jessica and moved around it. She raised her good arm to show him that she was harmless.

"Stop right there!" the man called out.

Jessica froze.

"What the hell you doin' on my land?"

"I'm just a drifter," Jessica lied. "I've been out here on my own a couple of days. I just saw you people and was hoping I could get some help. My shoulder is hurt and I haven't eaten in a couple of days. Please, could you help me?"

The man looked around. "Do I look like someone who

wants to help you? Get the fuck outta here!"

Pushing her luck, Jessica took a couple of steps forward. "Please, I won't stay long."

Then she heard the girl on the table scream, "Help me!" She sounded like a child.

"What's going on here?" Jessica asked.

The man reached around to the back of his pants and brought it out with a gun. He pointed it toward her and she heard the first shot go off, then ricochet off the ground nearby. Jessica stumbled back, falling onto the ground as another shot went off. She hurried to her feet and dove behind the brush. Forgetting about the dead bodies, she went to the ground next to them, and then turned and threw up.

Two more gunshots rang out, and then she heard the roaring engine of the truck behind her.

***

Will

The first gunshot had been hard to distinguish, but the ones that followed confirmed that Jessica was probably in trouble.

"Go! Go!" Gabriel yelled.

Will hung his head out the window and shouted, "Hang on!" to Marcus, who sat in the bed of the truck. In the back seat, Sarah cried and Holly cocked a pistol. Will punched the gas, the tires screeching on the asphalt, and raced toward the driveway.

He made the left turn onto the dirt path, barely slowing down and kicking up a cloud of dust behind them. Jessica was lying behind a bush, and he thought of stopping for her, but she waved him on and yelled, "Keep going!"

The truck reached the other side of the large bush and they found themselves out in the open. The long driveway led all the way up to an old barn, which sat near a large farmhouse. Just off the side of the path, he saw the small group of people standing around a table. They all looked toward him.

Then he saw something strange that made him stop the truck.

"Why did you stop?" Holly demanded.

He pointed toward the group and said to the passengers, "What the fuck is going on here?"

A girl screamed on the table. Nearby, a large man had an Empty trapped at the end of an animal control pole. The two groups just stared at each other. Will watched one of the men reach into his pocket and stuff something into the mouth of the girl on the table. Then he knelt behind the table, using the girl as a shield.

"What the fuck you doin' on my property?" the man shouted.

"We have reason to believe you may have someone we're looking for," Will replied.

"And what goddamn reason is that?"

"Did you kidnap a child? Dylan is his name."

The man laughed. "You've got to be fuckin' shittin' me. Y'all the ones that killed Trent and Cody?"

"We didn't kill them. You got duped into thinking so." Will swallowed. "Is David here, too?"

The man ignored the question. "Boy, if you don't get the fuck off my property right now, I guarantee you're going to regret it."

Will looked over to Gabriel, whose expression had turned cold.

"We aren't leaving," Gabriel said.

Will's sweaty palms gripped the steering wheel. He could feel his heart beating against his ribcage.

"Look, just give us the boy and let the girl on the table go. No one has to get hurt."

"No one gets hurt? That depends on you! Tell you what... you've got to the count of three to turn that piece of shit around and get the fuck off my land! If you don't, I can promise you some folk 'bout to get hurt!" the man threatened.

Will could feel all the eyes in the truck on him, awaiting his next move.

"One!"

He glanced into the mirror again and saw that Sarah was crying, the young nurse scared out of her mind. Holly's face was much more determined. Dylan had become like a much younger brother to her, and she wanted to get him back almost as much as Gabriel did.

"Two!"

Marcus remained in the bed of the truck, gun ready. But it was another look at Gabriel's face that confirmed Will's decision. It was a coldness Will hadn't seen in his friend. Dylan was here, and Gabriel was going to get him back no matter what. Then, a thought brought with it a chill. It was almost as if Will could feel that David was near. His eyes narrowed, and he turned his hand over and over again on the wheel.

"Three!"

***

David

By the time the first gunshot went off, David had made it halfway up the stairs. He turned around and shuffled back down to the first floor, hurrying to the front window. A truck raced toward the picnic table and his so-called associates. He'd started to reach for the door when he recognized one of the men in the back of the truck.

Marcus.

"Oh, shit."

David checked his waist to make sure he still had the Glock and the knife. Both were there, securely affixed to his side. The gunshots had attracted Cindy to the window and she now stood beside him.

"Son of a bitch," Cindy said.

The two girls who'd been sitting on the sofa watching television all morning had been unmoved from the gunshots outside. The front door opened and the two boys entered from the porch.

"Get to your fuckin' room," Cindy said to the two girls and the boys. "And lock the door. Don't let no one in, you hear me?" The kids hurried up the stairs. Cindy then looked over to David. "Wait here."

The woman hurried into a room on the other side of the living area. When she reappeared, she had a rifle over her shoulder and was checking to make sure a pistol in her hand was loaded.

"Go around back and head for the barn," David said. "You might be able to flank 'em if you go that way. I'll take the front."

The gap in the woman's teeth showed and she nodded. "Good idea."

She ran through the kitchen toward the back door. Before she fell out of sight, Cindy turned around and wished David luck. He acknowledged her with a nod, and then she disappeared.

David waited until he heard the back door open and close, and then instead of racing out the front door to help defend the farm, he turned and darted up the stairs.

Opening the various doors, he started to check the rooms. The first two he opened were vacant. Upon opening the third door, he came across the two girls who'd been looking out the window with him just moments earlier. They each sat staring at him from the edges of their respective beds. Without saying a word, he closed the door and tried the next room.

When he went to turn the knob to the next door, it was locked, and he noticed it was dead-bolted from the outside. He unlocked the door, swung it open, and found who he was looking for.

Dylan, the young child who'd been with Will and Marcus' group, lay on the bed, curled up and covering his ears. When he heard the door open, he sat up and stared at David.

"What's going on out there?" Dylan asked. "What do you want?"

Without a word, David hurried over and grabbed the boy.

"Stop! Leave me alone!" Dylan shouted, pounding his fists against David.

David sat the boy up straight on the bed. With one hand, he grasped Dylan's collar. With the other, he brought the cold barrel of the gun up to the child's nose.

"Listen to me. You're gonna shut your little fuckin' mouth and come with me, you got that? And if I hear one more peep outta you, I'm gonna clock you over the side of the head with this. Hell, I might just shoot you."

The boy's mouth fell open, and David could see from his expression that he understood. He grabbed the child by the wrist and dragged him out of the room.

Upon exiting, he headed for the stairs, pulling Dylan behind him. Just as he approached the top of the staircase, the front door swung open. David moved into a nearby doorway and covered the young boy's mouth before he could call out. He looked around the corner and down the stairs, and flashed a small grin when he saw who'd entered the house.

CHAPTER EIGHTEEN

<u>Gabriel</u>

"Give me some cover," Gabriel said.

At his request, Will had pulled up to the front of the house so Gabriel could run inside and search for Dylan. In the bed of the truck, Marcus had ducked down, exchanging fire with the men on the other side of the yard.

Will readied a rifle and Marcus did the same in the bed of the truck, preparing to provide cover for Gabriel to run inside the house. In the back seat, Holly worked to try and calm Sarah down.

"Go!" Will shouted.

Gabriel swung open the door of the truck as Will and Marcus fired. He looked toward the door and made a run for it. Shots ricocheted off one of the beams that held up the patio, chipping away a chunk of the painted white wood. He reached the front door and found cover.

He knelt down by the door as Will turned the truck around, gunshots continuing to ping off the side of it, and headed toward the middle of the yard.

Gabriel opened the front door.

***

Just inside the house, he saw that the bottom floor appeared to be empty. To his left, Gabriel saw an old dining room table and a kitchen with dirty dishes stacked as tall as him sitting in the sink. In the other direction, an old beat-up couch sat in front of an old tube television. Directly in front of him was a set of stairs.

Gabriel stood in front of the staircase, unsure whether to check the top or the bottom level of the house. Gunshots rang outside, urging him to make a decision.

He took a deep breath and mounted the first step. The faded wooden stairs creaked as he walked, showing their age. He moved carefully, trying to mute his steps, but it was of no use.

Once he reached the top of the stairs, Gabriel took a moment to scan the long, slender hallway. Doors were set into either wall, each one closed. The floor was made up of more of the same old, wood paneling, photos on the wall looking like they hadn't been dusted in years. He held the pistol up in front of his face, ready to fire at any threat he came across.

He opened the door nearest him and moved through the entrance quickly, his finger itching the trigger. Though the room look to have been occupied recently, with blankets and sheets a mess on the bed and clothes tossed on the floor next to it, the room was vacant.

Gabriel moved to the next room, opening the door to reveal an empty bathroom.

His heart raced, knowing that at any moment he could open one of the doors and be face to face with someone ready to hurt him. On the flip side, he could find Dylan, who he knew had to be in the house somewhere. He was tempted to call to him.

The game that was becoming a kind of Russian roulette continued when he opened the next door. Gabriel peeked inside to see two teenage girls sitting on the edge of two beds. They wore identical outfits, each with the same stoic expression across their faces. Neither girl even flinched when Gabriel entered.

He started to speak, but one of the girls slowly raised her arm and pointed out into the hallway.

He moved to the side and turned around to see a door. When he looked back to the young girl, she still pointed out to the hallway, directly at the same door.

"Is there a boy in there?" he asked.

Neither girl responded, but the other girl now lifted up her arm and pointed to the same place.

Gabriel turned out of the room and moved across the hallway. He reached for the handle, turned it, and pulled. His eyes widened.

"Dylan."

The boy sat on the floor of a small linen closet, not making a noise. He wasn't tied up or gagged, so Gabriel assumed he had been hiding.

"Let's get you out of here."

Just as Gabriel leaned down to pick the boy up, the floor creaked and he heard a forceful grunt. He turned just in time to see David Ellis lunging at him with a knife. Gabriel dodged, avoiding most the blow, but the knife still grazed his shoulder blade, ripping his shirt and cutting him so that he grimaced.

David struck again, leaving Gabriel no time to tend to his wound. This time, Gabriel managed to roll out of the way, causing David to miss all together. But in the process, Gabriel's gun fell from his waist, sliding into the open room with the two young girls.

When he got to his feet, he stood less than ten feet away from David. Gabriel had no weapon left, while David tossed his knife from hand to hand. Looking to David's belt, Gabriel noticed that the man also carried a handgun.

"I'm gonna enjoy butchering you," David said.

Gabriel fought for each breath. His back was to the dead end of the hall, and he was looking toward the stairs beyond David. Behind him were rooms he'd yet to check, and for all he knew, there could be others waiting in there, and he'd be surrounded. David lunged toward him, and when Gabriel gasped and jumped back, David laughed.

"This is gonna be way too fuckin' easy," David said.

Raising the knife, David came at Gabriel.

Gabriel's eyes went wide, and he was able to maneuver away from the blow. He ended up beside David and punched him in the kidney. David winced, then turned toward Gabriel and stabbed at him again. Gabriel caught David's wrist, then used his free hand to grab David's shirt at the shoulder and drive him against the wall. David struggled to try and use his free hand to punch Gabriel, but he fought it off, all the while managing to keep the knife from driving into him. Feeling like he was about to lose leverage, Gabriel brought his knee up into David's gut, which was enough of a shock to make the man drop the knife.

Gabriel pulled at David and then jammed him against the wall on the opposite side of the hallway. With David stunned,

Gabriel delivered a blow directly below his left eye. It only managed to hold David back for a moment, as he reared back and delivered his own right hook, connecting with the side of Gabriel's face.

The two men now found themselves engaged in a fist fight, trading punches and throwing each other against the walls to each side, both men bleeding from their cheeks.

Ducking a hook, David was able to grab the back of Gabriel's head and slam him against the wall. Gabriel could hear his own nose crunch against the drywall, and it felt like the entire thing turned inside-out and drove into his brain. He crumbled to the ground.

Gabriel writhed on the wooden floor, blood pooling from his nostrils. He put his hand to his face, and it came back crimson. Then he felt an intense pain in his ribcage as David kicked him in his left side.

"You're fucking useless," David said, spitting down at the ground right next to Gabriel.

Gabriel curled into a ball, clutching his side. He felt the blood continue to pour from his broken nose, collecting on the wooden floor. He struggled to breathe, fighting for every breath as his lungs felt like they punched at his beaten ribs. When he heard a click, he looked up.

David stood over him, the barrel of a Glock pointed squarely at his head. David's mouth crescendoed into a smile as their eyes met.

"I should have already done this when I had the chance," David said. "At least I got to kick your ass around a bit before watching you die."

Gabriel tensed every muscle in his body, closed his eyes,

and looked away. He thought of Katie and Sarah. He wondered if they were still out there somewhere, trying to survive like he was. Were they waiting for him? Were they out trying to find him? Then, another thought came to him. He pondered whether his beautiful wife and daughter might, perhaps, be awaiting him in the afterlife.

As these questions held his focus, Gabriel heard a yell and then felt the weight of someone on top of him. He grimaced again, his body still aching from the fight.

"Boy, you better get the hell outta the way right now," David said.

David glared at Dylan, who shielded Gabriel's body.

"Please, don't hurt him," Dylan said.

David scoffed, and then Gabriel, barely able to look up from the ground, felt the boy begin to struggle as David worked to pull him off the injured man beneath him.

The weight of Dylan left Gabriel, and he looked up to see David clutching the boy with his free hand while he reacquainted the barrel of the Glock with its target.

A gunshot sounded, and Gabriel flinched, closing his eyes and awaiting an intense pain—a burn.

But he didn't feel anything.

The gunshot hadn't come from David's gun. Gabriel looked up to see David looking back and forth between his target and something behind him. He'd finally let Dylan go, but now held him by the arm at his side.

Gabriel fought to look around David, and he finally saw where the shot had come from.

The two young girls who'd been sitting in the room now stood side by side, just outside the doorway. One of them, the older looking of the two, had Gabriel's handgun fixed on David.

"Sweetie, put the gun down," David said in a cordial manner.

The girl ignored David, keeping the gun pointed at him.

"Hand over the gun. I won't hurt you."

David reached out to try and wrangle the gun from the child, and Gabriel startled when the gun went off again. She'd shot just beyond David, seemingly missing him on purpose once more as another warning, and blowing a hole in the wall just behind Gabriel. Gabriel hoped it would be his last warning.

"No more killing," the girl not holding the weapon, said. "Leave." Her tone was mumbled and gentle.

David looked back down toward Gabriel and scowled. He backed away, heading towards the stairs. Dylan cried out for Gabriel, and David covered the boy's mouth. The girls apparently didn't care if David took the child; they just wouldn't allow Gabriel to die here in front of them.

"Not gonna be so lucky next time," David said.

Gabriel scratched at the wood floor, trying desperately to make it to his feet. Even with his mouth muted, Dylan continued to cry a muffled scream. But Gabriel didn't have it in him to get to stand.

He watched David and Dylan disappear down the stairs, and then he passed out.

CHAPTER NINETEEN

<u>David</u>

Once downstairs, David contemplated heading out the front door. Will's truck was now parked in the center of the yard, a straight line from the front porch, and the two groups were still trading fire. He decided to try and sneak around the back so as to not be seen.

When they arrived at the back door, only a screen door stood between them and the outside as gunshots continued to sing through the cool Autumn air. He pushed through the door and poked his head around the corner.

A line of tall bushes sat ten yards from the back door, stretching beyond the width of the large farmhouse. He scanned the area, noticing that it was clear. When he looked down to his left, he could see a pickup truck sitting behind the barn. It was Clint's truck. He'd ridden in it himself, so he knew that it ran.

Jackpot.

"Come on," he said, tugging on Dylan's arm.

"Where are you taking me?"

"Disney World. Come on."

David tightened his grip on the boy's forearm and pulled him down the stairs. He crept toward the corner of the house, then poked his head around the wall to look out toward the firefight. Danny, Clint, and Horace hid behind the large tree, which was luckily thick enough at its base to shield all three men. Halfway between the tree and the farmhouse sat the hospital group's truck. The cab appeared empty, but Marcus, Holly, and Will crouched down on the driver's side, using the vehicle as a shield from oncoming gunfire. He watched Marcus peak over the bed of the truck and fire toward the hillbillies, narrowly missing Danny.

From where David stood, he could take a shot at Will. He was a damn good shot, and even with a Glock, he'd have at least a small chance of hitting him. He pointed the gun toward him, cocking the weapon in preparation. His finger itched at the trigger, one eye closed tight as he took aim. Right as he'd started to squeeze, he put the gun down and decided against taking the shot. *Not yet.*

No, he had a much better idea.

***

Will

Will waited for the men to reload before peeking over the hood of the truck and shooting back. He fired off four rounds, then ducked back out of sight.

"Shit! Sarah!" Holly said.

The nurse had been given instructions to follow Holly's lead out of the truck. Instead, she still lay inside, screaming as gunfire continued to fly overhead and slam against the passenger side.

"She's gotta get out of there before they fire a round heavy enough to pierce through the panel and hit her," Marcus said.

"Sarah," Will said, shouting, "you've got to get out of the truck, now!"

The nurse continued to wail.

"Shit," Marcus said.

Marcus turned around toward the truck and reached through the doorway. He grabbed Sarah by her ankle.

"Sarah, sweetie, you've got to get out of the truck."

Will wished he'd just left Sarah back at the hospital. They desperately needed every set of hands they could have for the fight, but having the terrified nurse around was futile.

She finally stopped the constant wail, only yelling out when a heavy shot went off.

"Come on!" Marcus shouted.

Apparently confused, Sarah sat up.

"No!" Marcus called.

A single shot from a rifle sounded off, and there was a grotesque thud. Will looked into the truck just in time to see Sarah's head splatter all over the windows inside. Her body fell forward and her arms dangled out the door. The open door blocked Will's view of the rest of Sarah, but he could see her blood pouring down onto the ground.

Marcus turned away, moving back to his position by the rear tire.

"Goddammit!"

Will clenched his eyes shut for just a moment before he regained his focus. Somehow, the driver's side window was still in tact. He stood in a crouched position and moved around Holly to the driver's side front door, rising until he could look through the window.

"What can you see?" Holly asked.

"Two of the men are hiding behind that tree," Will said. "Then there's a shack twenty yards or so off to the left, and that big asshole is using that as cover."

Will ducked back behind the truck.

"Did you see the girl or the Empty?" Marcus asked, yelling over the gunfire.

As soon as there was a break in the fire, Will rose again to where his eyes could just look through the window. He scanned the yard, looking for the Empty, but it had apparently disappeared. He then looked back toward the table. He could see it shaking. Apparently, whoever—or whatever—was bound there was struggling on the other side. Will ducked all the way out of view again.

"I'm not sure where the Empty went," Will said. "Maybe they shot it, but I don't see a body." And the table is moving. That girl could still be alive on the other side. We've gotta do whatever we can to make sure we don't hit her."

The gunfire came to a halt.

It became so quiet that Will could hear the girl struggling on the table. He hoped that one of the men wouldn't get tired of her writhing and shoot her.

"No one needs to get hurt," one of the men shouted. "Put down your weapons."

"Where's Dylan?" Will yelled back.

"Who?"

"The boy! Where's the boy?"

Will heard feet moving through the grass near the tree. Marcus had apparently heard it, too, as he poked his head around the back of the truck. Will rose again to look through the cab of the truck. A skinny man with long hair was making a bee-line for the large barn.

Marcus put the rifle to his shoulder and took aim. He was

able to do so at an angle where the other two men couldn't see him setting up a shot.

Will covered his ears, and Holly did the same.

The shot went off.

A yell.

Marcus withdrew the gun and retreated back to his resting position.

"Son of a bitch!" the man who'd been trying to negotiate yelled.

The two remaining men opened up fire again on the pickup truck.

There was another break in the shooting, and Will looked over to Marcus.

"Helluva shot."

"Thanks."

"They've gotta run out of ammo soon," Holly said.

"You'd think so," Will said. "Let's just make sure we make our shots count." He looked over to Holly. "Do like Marcus did and see if you can peek around the front bumper while keeping most of your body protected behind the truck. Keep an eye on the guy behind the shack and see if you can hit him. Jessica is still off in that bush somewhere, but I think they've forgotten about her. Make sure he doesn't make a run for her." Then he looked over to Marcus. "Try to keep an eye on the house in case someone is in there. It's doubtful, because I'm sure they'd have come out by now. Other than that, set up over the top of the truck bed, and fire at whichever one of these assholes you can get a good shot at. I'm gonna stay focused on Boss Man behind the tree."

They each took their positions, and the firefight

continued.

***

Gunfire be damned, David reached the vehicle behind the barn, unscathed. He dragged Dylan over and opened the unlocked passenger side door. He pushed the boy inside.

"Stay here. I've got no issue putting a bullet in your back if you decide to try something funny."

David slammed the door and hurried around to the driver's side. He opened up the door and sat in the driver's seat. Rummaging around for keys, he checked under the visor, in the armrest, and in the glove box. A key was nowhere to be found. It was an older model sedan, so he figured he should have no problem jump-starting it. So, he stepped out and kneeled down, leaning into the floorboard.

A short time later, the car roared to life.

David stood, about to step into the vehicle when he heard rustling in the nearby brush. He turned to face the tree-line and drew his Glock. He crept toward the sound, working to tune out the fight happening in front of the barn. He heard a weep and the plants rustled again. David moved around a bush, and saw a figure lying down, trying to hide. He cocked his gun.

It was Samuel, the preacher.

"Please, don't hurt me. I just want to get out of here," Samuel said, pleading.

"How the fuck did you get back here?" David asked.

The preacher put up his hands, both of them trembling.

Another noise caught David's attention, and he turned. It sounded as if it had come from the other side of the barn.

"Please, don't—"

The boy hit the passenger side window and yelled something from the front seat of the vehicle. Samuel narrowed his eyes.

"What's going on?" Samuel asked.

"Shut your mouth," David hissed at the preacher. He shook his head, then turned and crept toward the back of the barn.

He put his back up against the rear of the building, and slowly shuffled toward the corner. Shadows covered the backside of the barn, the sun starting to settle down for sleep. A cool breeze snuck through the tree-line. As he approached the corner, he heard the sound of something wiggling in the tall grass again, and whatever it was growled. He tensed, holding a strong grip on the Glock. His heart beat against his chest, and he felt the urge to destroy creep up into his gut again. This was it. He'd fulfill that need again.

Just as he started around the corner, he heard a snarl, and the creature lunged at him. It howled, diving straight at David's arm. He never saw it coming until it was on him.

The Empty, still dragging the pole looped around its neck, sunk its teeth into David's forearm, just above the wrist. Before it had the chance to tear away the skin, David pressed the barrel of the handgun to the thing's temple and pulled the trigger.

He fell to the ground, gasping for air.

Shit. Oh, shit.

David sat with his back against the rear wall of the barn, pressing his palm down against the wound. His mind raced and he felt lightheaded. Footsteps approached from the brush, and he looked up to see the preacher at his side.

"Oh, no," Samuel said.

The preacher dashed to the car, grabbing a shop towel that sat on the trunk.

"Here," he said. Samuel wrapped the towel around David's arm, tying it taut.

David's heart raced faster as his mind panicked. He couldn't believe he'd been so careless.

"Help me up," David requested.

Samuel grabbed onto David's good arm, and leaned down to help him to his feet. David grimaced, having to use his bitten arm to help push himself off the ground. On his feet, he headed for the driver's side of the vehicle.

"Get in the back," David said.

Samuel narrowed his eyes. "You can't drive. And where will you take me?"

"We're gonna get away from this shithole and you're gonna fix this."

"But, sir, I—"

David drew the Glock and aimed it at Samuel's head. "I ain't got nothin' to lose. I'll kill ya." He loaded a round into the chamber, circling his lips with his tongue. "Now, you better jump in the back seat of this car right now, or I'll pull this damn trigger. Don't test me, priest."

Hands raised, Samuel did as he was told and stepped through the back door.

David stumbled into the cab, his lightheadedness subsiding. His arm burned as if it were aflame. He tried to bury the pain in the back of his mind—along with the thought that he would soon turn into an Empty—as he shifted the column shift down into drive.

"Are you sure you're okay to drive?" Samuel asked.

"Just lay down, preacher."

David pressed the pedal to the floor, and the car shot around the side of the barn.

***

Will

The large man dropped to the ground behind the shack like a demolished building, as Will's aim with the rifle had been true. The cowardly man who'd been hiding behind the tree, now left alone with his two protectors laying dead under the shadow of the branches, scampered away toward the neighboring house.

Will stepped out into the open from behind the truck and took aim at the running man.

He clenched his eye.

He fired.

Miss.

Will stepped a few yards closer, and then fired once more. This one hit.

The man fell forward, toppling into the tall grass.

Will had looked down to reload his weapon just in case the man stood again, when he heard panting. He looked up and the girl who'd been on the table stood, looking in his direction.

"Hey," he yelled to her.

The girl ran toward the barn.

Just as he was about to chase her, he glanced to the side as he heard the roar of an engine coming from the back of the property. He turned his head and saw another vehicle heading right for them. Will would have recognized the man driving from a mile away.

David.

Will stepped away from the van, moving directly into the path of the oncoming vehicle. At the speed it raced toward him, he figured he had one shot. He raised the rifle flush against his shoulder, looking down the barrel and aiming at his target. For the first time, he noticed Dylan in the passenger seat. He didn't care. There was no way he'd miss. The car moved in a straight line, bouncing up and down on the dirt, but not enough to hinder Will's aim.

The gun clicked as the bullet readied for flight.

Will drew in a deep breath.

The vehicle was only yards away now.

"Fuck you."

Right as Will squeezed the trigger, someone pushed him, and he found himself rolling on the ground. The shot went off, and right after the loud bang came from the rifle, he heard a grotesque thud, followed by a scream.

The car raced by, having missed him.

Will turned and started to fire another round, until he thought better of it. The car was now swerving, and he didn't have a clear shot at the driver. God forbid he fire the rifle and accidentally hit Dylan.

His attention was drawn to where he'd just stood when he heard Holly crying. He looked over and his eyes went wide. The gun fell from his hands.

Marcus.

Will hurried to Marcus' side, sliding across the grass on his knees. Blood covered Marcus and the ground surrounding him. Will's attention went to Marcus' face first, seeing that the eyes were open but vacant. His guts spilled from his torn and open stomach, the victim of an apparent hit and run. Will understood what Marcus had done. Even had Will's shot connected with David and killed him, the vehicle likely would have still bowled over him. Marcus had many times told Will that he owed him for saving his life back at Ellis Metals, and now he'd paid his unnecessary debt by sacrificing his own life, getting run over by his former friend and boss.

Everything around Will went black. Holly became a muted figure, her mouth moving, tears running down her face, no sound coming out.

Will passed his hand over Marcus' eyes, closing them. He unsheathed the knife from his side, and drew in a deep breath.

"I'm so sorry."

Will shut his eyes and thrusted the knife into the side of Marcus' head. Behind him, Holly screamed.

Will then got to his feet and retreated back to where he'd dropped the rifle. He picked it up and marched back over to the truck.

The passenger side door was open and he threw the rifle on the seat, shutting the door. Will then walked around to the driver's side and got into the cab, cranking up the truck. Holly came to the window.

"Don't do this," she pleaded. "Wait on Gabriel, and let's go find them together."

"Back away from the truck, Holly."

"Will, please."

"Go find Gabriel and stay put. I'll be back with Dylan."

"Please, baby, don't—"

"Now!"

The sheer volume of his voice was enough to make Holly jump back, and he threw the truck into drive and punched the gas, throwing up dirt behind him as the wheels spun in place before the truck took off. He cut the wheel, flipping the truck around.

The pickup raced down the driveway, and he was in pursuit.

CHAPTER TWENTY

David

The two lane backroad was mostly a flat, straight path. Trees lined either side, acting as a blockade to the homes that lay hidden off the street behind them. If the road had been a trek of voluptuous curves, he'd likely have wrecked by now, running the vehicle off the road into the trees.

David could hardly see, his vision really starting to falter.

Sweat pooled on his forehead, and the wound on his arm, still wrapped taught with a shop towel, throbbed underneath its covering. He couldn't be sure if it was because the makeshift tourniquet had been wrapped so tight, or if it was because the massive hole in his arm was slowly coming alive.

In the back seat, Samuel mumbled something to himself. The boy in the passenger seat asked all sorts of questions, but David simply ignored him. In his current condition, it would've been hard enough to drive without the blabbering child riding shotgun, and a few times he nearly swung the back of his arm at Dylan in an attempt to knock him out cold. Instead, he focused on the road and blocked out the scared child.

As the car hit 70 mph, his heart raced. The dense population in these parts made for a clear path, as he hadn't seen any Empties or straggling survivors on this desolate road. Now, he just needed to find a good place to stop.

Pulling into one of the many driveways off the road was out of the question; they were out in the country, and he didn't want to come face to face with some survivalist protecting his land at all costs. Perhaps there would be somewhere up the road—maybe a church or a gas station—that he could pull into and hide the car behind, in case Will or anyone in his group followed them. He needed to find a place with plenty of open space for the preacher to try and draw this disease out of him, but he felt as if he might be running out of time.

A not-so-distant roar caught David's attention, and he looked in the rearview mirror to see headlights on a fast approaching vehicle.

Will.

David gritted his teeth, feeling another jolt of pain shoot up his arm. He fumbled his hand down to the A/C dial, cranking it up. Sweat bled through his clothes. Behind him, the truck gained on them. David punched the gas, watching the red dial swing up to 80.

David saw two versions of the same road in front of him, both moving in a blurred motion. He'd often driven after a night of having a few beers with friends, but had never experienced anything like this. If this had been a night in the old world and a cop had pulled him over, he likely would have just crumbled to the ground and passed out when the officer asked him to walk in a straight line.

The pursuing vehicle shot around to the side of David, who looked over and confirmed that it was Will manning the truck. Will's mouth moved, but David was unable to hear what he was yelling. All sound around him had diminished.

Will turned the truck into the side of David's vehicle.

David nearly lost control, but managed to keep a straight path. He turned the wheel, returning the assault back onto Will.

The impact caused Will to lose control.

Will's vehicle spun when David rammed into it near the rear tire. His hearing returned as both Dylan and Samuel screamed. Smoke from burning rubber clouded David's vision. He slammed on the brakes, but Will's truck spun in front of him, and David rammed into its passenger side door.

David cut the wheel and then blacked out just as the car went airborne into a ditch.

***

<u>Will</u>

The hood of the truck had folded like an accordion. Smoke rose from the engine, and there was a gentle hiss which sounded like air being slowly released from a punctured beach ball. Will came to, his head pounding. He reached for his left temple, and immediately felt the bump around where the throb originated from. The window was still intact, but he assumed his head had crashed into it during the accident, thus knocking him out.

He sat up straight and looked around. His truck had gone off the road, landing on its side in a ditch. His driver's side door had been pinned against the ground, making it near impossible to escape. Will unbuckled his seatbelt, thankful he had decided to put it on, and climbed up and over to the passenger seat, pulling the handle and pushing the door open, then using its frame and his upper-body strength to pull himself out of the vehicle.

Once he was out, he rolled onto the road, feeling the pain

in his ribs for the first time as his adrenaline began wearing off. It didn't feel as if anything was broken or punctured, but it hurt for him to breathe.

Will lay on his stomach, palms flat on the asphalt. As he pushed himself up, he saw the other vehicle folded up near a tree. Smoke rose from the folded front end. David had apparently hit the tree at high speed.

He held his breath.

Dylan.

Praying that the boy would be okay, Will stumbled to his feet.

His knee ached, and upon the first step, he felt the sharp pain hit his stomach, sinking through to his ribs. He was forced to gasp just to gather a single breath. He lumbered toward the car, working to catch a glance of the boy on the other side of the battered, smoking hood.

When the cab finally came into view, the front windshield was almost nonexistent, and Will saw Dylan still strapped into the passenger seat, blood showing on his head. Through the driver's side back window, he could see the man who'd been riding in the back seat—slumped over, but still fastened into the seat he'd occupied.

Will's eyes narrowed.

The driver's seat was empty.

He twisted and looked at the road. About twenty yards from where the vehicle had stopped, a puddle of blood glistened off the asphalt in the shape of a kidney bean. Tiny streams flowed away from its nucleus, leading down the slight incline and into the ditch off the side of the road.

But there wasn't a body.

Will trudged toward the blood lake, reaching down to draw his weapon from its holster. He practically had to carry his right leg as he walked, the pain from the accident intensifying.

The trail of blood flowed off the road and appeared to lead into a collection of trees, and a dissatisfying thought fell upon Will.

Had David died in the accident?

David Ellis didn't deserve that. He'd earned the right to die a slow and torturous death at the hands of Will himself. Will hadn't come through all this just to find the man who'd killed his mother lying in a ditch, unmoved, having gone to hell while basking in mother nature.

Monsters deserve to suffer.

As he lumbered toward the brush, the bushes rustled and leaves stirred on the ground. Will scoffed a kind of relieved and tired laugh. *He's still alive.*

Will stopped to make sure the gun was loaded, and then he thought of something. With the amount of blood on the ground, there was no way that David would have enough strength or be conscious enough to fight back. No, Will wouldn't have to make it *too* fast, though he wondered how many more breaths David would be able to inhale, considering how much blood he'd lost. Either way, Will slipped the gun back into its holster and drew the knife from his hip. Examining the blade in front of his face, what was left of the day's sun glared off the sharp tip as if to tell him it would be over soon, and that the weapon was here to carry out his wish. He thought of his mother, and her screams as that beast had torn into her. David, laughing in Will's ear, forcing him to watch.

He was ready.

This was it. Retribution.

Will followed the path of the blood down into the shallow ditch and on into the grass. More of the iron substance gleamed off the grass, leading behind a bush.

He gripped the knife, sweat gushing from the pores in his palms and wetting the handle of the knife.

Will drew a deep breath and stepped around the bush.

He cocked his head.

Nothing was there.

He looked back to the road to check that he'd followed the path correctly, and this one simple mistake distracted him long enough for the beast to strike.

A snarl came from behind a nearby tree, and Will turned just as an Empty launched itself at him and dug its teeth into his exposed arm, just above the elbow at his bicep. The knife fell from Will's grasp and he screamed. He clenched his teeth as he grimaced and pushed the creature off of him. Will's hand went immediately to the wound on his arm, and his eyes widened when he looked up.

Even through the pale eyes and tattered skin, there was no mistaking the identity of the Empty: it was David.

Will reached for his gun, but with his body still recovering from the accident, his draw wasn't quick enough. David made another dive at him, knocking the weapon from his hand. The creature's teeth snapped, and Will grabbed onto its shirt, throwing it down to the ground. The momentum caused Will to stumble, and he fell into the nearby ditch.

He looked up and saw the creature working its way up to

its knees. When Will tried to stand again, he slipped in the mud on the slight incline of the shallow ditch. He fell and his knee slammed down onto a rock the size of a tennis ball. The pain from the already hurting joint shot to his brain and he clutched his leg, instinctively writhing on the ground.

He looked up just as David, mouth wide, pounced on him. Will tried to roll out of the way, but the thing already had ahold of him. Will lay with his back pressing into the mud as the monster clicked its jaws, saliva dripping from the bottom lip.

Mud covered Will's palm, and it became slick enough for his hand to entirely lose its grip on David's shoulder.

The creature's weight shifted down onto Will, and it buried its teeth into his shoulder.

Will screamed again.

This was it. He was going to lie in this ditch and be eaten alive by the human monster turned supernatural beast that had killed his mother. Somehow, through all his panic, Will found a very brief moment to wonder whether any part of David Ellis' human mind was still intact. Was he completely vanished from the world? Or did he have any sort of realization that he was on top of Will, ending his life at this moment? Was the bastard enjoying this?

Will couldn't muster the energy to fight back. Pinned down in the mud, he closed his eyes, just trying to focus on something that wasn't the pain or the thought of impending death.

A thundering bang filled the space in the air, and the snarling in Will's ear stopped. All the weight of his assailant fell on top of him, and the pain of teeth digging into his flesh was replaced by a sudden panic that he had to fight for air.

"Help," a voice said.

He heard the plea, but the gunmetal sky above slowly faded to black, like the end of a dramatic movie about to roll the credits.

The two wounds on his arm pulsated, the pain intense. Everything went dark.

***

Jessica

Shadows of the night draped over the pale asphalt, and Jessica ran as fast as she could. She wasn't quite sure why she'd started running from the farm. Something, a premonition perhaps, had urged her not to wait for Will to return. It had encouraged her to take chase and run after him.

In the distance, she heard the cries.

"Help!"

It sounded like the voice of a child, apparently pleading for someone, anyone, to help.

As she passed over a small hill, the scene of the accident came into sight. It was almost as if her legs churned faster and with more urgency now, like a conductor throwing coal over an engine. She saw both of the vehicles on the side of the road, one jammed against a tree and the other rolled onto its side in a nearby ditch. And as her feet slapped the concrete, the young boy appeared from between the two trucks, waving her down.

"Help! Please!" he called out. The boy was jumping up and down, pulling at his hair. Panic colored his voice.

A man sat in the back seat of the car, and with her vision

bouncing up and down with the rhythm of her sprint, she was unable to tell if he was moving or not. All she wanted was to reach the boy and see why he'd called for help. In the back of her mind, she feared the worst.

That fear reared its ugly face when she finally saw what the boy had been crying about.

Will.

He lay facing up to the coming darkness above, his stomach rising up and down at a more frantic pace than it should have been. A stilled body pinned one of his arms to the ground, laying halfway up the limb. Jessica slowed to something between a walk and a stand-still. Will's eyes were open, but they looked lifeless. They looked... empty.

She hurried to his side and pushed the body of the dead creature the rest of the way off of him.

His other arm folded across his chest, and she saw the two open wounds pulsating.

"He got bit," Dylan said, wiping his eyes.

Jessica looked to the body she'd just pushed off of Will. Blood pooled from a hole in one of his cheeks, and his pale eyes seemed to look up at her. She remembered his face from the hospital; it was David.

She refocused her attention to Will.

Grabbing his hand, she watched as he continued to fight for air. He stared with wide eyes, as if he was looking past the darkening sky. Like he was being pulled somewhere—out of this body, out of this life.

"Stay with me," she said, his face in her palm.

For the first time, he looked up at her. He looked so scared, yet as if he wasn't sure he was even looking at her.

She felt a chill stretch through her body.

His mouth moved, but the dialogue was inaudible.

"What?" Jessica asked.

She put her ear down close to his face.

"It's beautiful," he mumbled.

Tears rolled down her face. "Don't. Stay here, Will. Don't you leave us."

Still gripping his hand, she moved their hands down to his stomach, where she could feel his stomach rising and falling much more slowly now.

"So beautiful." Will hissed, reaching to taste another breath.

When the gasp had passed, his stomach fell and she waited for it to rise again. Jessica looked into his eyes, and he appeared to be staring past her now, over her shoulder. He didn't make a noise.

And his stomach didn't rise again.

CHAPTER TWENTY-ONE

Jessica

The sun had almost completely hidden behind the horizon now, and it would soon be pitch black outside. They wouldn't be able to stay here much longer. But Jessica couldn't leave his side.

Will was dead.

She lay over his body, the side of her head pressed against his stomach. The only thing she was conscious of was staying clear of the open wounds, not sure if the bite could somehow spread to her. She couldn't stop crying, and her weeps were loud and unforgiving. She was so distraught that she'd completely forgotten about the young boy, and she finally looked up when she heard him sniffle.

Dylan sat on his legs in the middle of the road, a stark face absent of emotion. She scurried to her feet and went to him.

Kneeling down, she hugged him.

"Dylan, I'm so sorry."

The boy didn't hug her back and he didn't respond. She pulled away to look him in the face, and she concluded that the child was in shock. He then looked her dead in the eyes.

"When will he change?" Dylan mumbled.

Oh, shit.

Through all her grief, Jessica hadn't even thought about

the fact that Will would soon turn into one of the creatures. There hadn't seemed to be a set timetable on how quickly people had changed: it had varied from person to person, based on her little experience seeing the transformation happen.

"We've gotta get back to the farm," Jessica said.

"No!" Dylan cried.

He ran over to Will and hugged him.

Jessica trembled, her palms sweating. Will could change at any moment. She chewed on her nails, knowing she'd would have to pry the distraught child away from his friend.

"We can't stay here, sweetie. It's not safe. He's going to...." She cut herself off.

"Maybe we can help him," Dylan pleaded. "Please, we can't leave him."

Jessica's eyes filled and she reached down to grab Dylan.

"I'm so sorry, honey. We have to leave him. He's dangerous."

"No!" Dylan shouted.

A voice then came from behind her. Jessica turned, and she saw a trembling hand sticking out of one of the windows of the vehicle, followed by another groan. She rose from her kneel and hurried over.

The man was still strapped into the back seat. His eyes were slightly open, his lips parted as he gasped. When he saw Jessica, he dropped his arm.

"Please, get me out of here," he said, barely able to speak above his heavy breathing.

Jessica opened the door and reached over to unfasten the seatbelt. As soon as it released, the man slumped over.

"You have to take me over to him," the man said. "Please."

Jessica narrowed her eyes. "What?"

"Please. Take me over to him."

"How?" she asked. "Can you walk?"

Gently, the man shook his head. "I'm not sure."

For whatever reason, Jessica didn't question the man as to why he needed to be taken to Will. Something inside just told her to do as the man asked.

"Dylan," she said sharply. The boy looked up from Will, his once stoic face now red from tears. "I need you right now!'

Dylan rose to his feet, then scurried over to the car as he apparently realized the urgency in the situation.

"You have to help me get him over to Will."

"Why?"

"Just help me!" Jessica demanded. "Let's see if we can slide him off the seat."

Jessica could see the man's pain as he gritted his teeth together, his eyes closed. He groaned the entire time, but they were able to slide him off the seat. His feet hit the ground, and the man grimaced as they sat him up.

"Can you walk?" Jessica asked.

"I think so," he responded. "Please, just help me."

Jessica grabbed ahold of his arm and threw it around her, holding his hand on her shoulder. Dylan was too short to mirror Jessica from the other side, but he walked next to the man to help brace him. The man walked like an elderly person with a cane, his back obviously having been injured during the accident.

They came around the front of the vehicle where Will still lay unmoved. Jessica feared he'd have turned by now, and was relieved that there appeared to still be time for the man to possibly help him, given that that seemed to be his intention.

"What's your name?" Jessica finally asked, as they were halfway to Will now.

"S-Samuel," the man replied.

For no reason, Jessica didn't give her name, and Samuel didn't ask. Perhaps it was because they were both so focused on just trying to get him across the road.

"I need to be on the side of his body where the bite is," he said.

"There are two," Jessica informed him.

"Same arm?"

She nodded.

"Good."

They reached Will, and Jessica wished she had closed his eyes before she'd hurried over to Samuel. They looked up toward the sky, having been abandoned by life inside. It was difficult for her to even look at him.

Samuel managed to kneel next to Will, and he looked back up to Jessica.

"I'm not sure what is going to happen, but you have to make me a promise."

"What?" Jessica asked.

"That you'll kill me if I change."

Jessica narrowed her eyes. "What? No."

"Please," Samuel said. "Please, promise. We are running out of time."

Jessica hesitated, looking down to Will's lifeless body. She looked again at Samuel and nodded.

"Thank you," Samuel said. "Now, stand back."

"What are you doing?" Dylan asked.

Jessica took the boy's hand and walked back toward the center of the road. She stopped when they were just over five yards back.

Samuel placed his hands on Will's injured arm and closed his eyes. His mouth began to move, but Jessica couldn't hear what he said. The wind blew harder, and the dark sky reflected a smoke tint that signaled it could open up again and rain down on them. Samuel's mouth ceased moving and he opened his eyes, looking straight ahead.

"What's he doing?" Dylan whispered.

"Shh," Jessica urged in return.

Reaching under his shirt to his chest, Samuel grasped onto something as he began to speak. The words were indistinguishable.

One time when she'd been a teenager, Jessica had visited one of those churches where the preacher and the congregation would randomly speak in tongues. The noises spilling from the man's mouth now sounded no different. Samuel raised his free hand to the sky as he looked up, his eyes closing again.

The first new drop of rain fell from the sky and, within moments, heaven seemed to open as thunder sounded in the distance. The rain came down, and Samuel looked as if he were bathing in it, though Jessica wondered if he was even aware it had started to storm.

Dylan hugged Jessica tight, and she looked down at him.

A new sense of fear painted his face as he worked to hide his eyes.

"What's happening?" he asked.

The question drew Jessica's attention back to Will and Samuel, and her mouth fell agape.

Will's body shook. At first, she thought it was possibly her eyes playing tricks on her. But she made herself stand completely still, confirming the truth. It wasn't an intense tremble, but he was moving, apparently involuntarily. His eyes still had the same vacant look to them, staring up at the sky.

Samuel talked louder in the same scattered language. All the fear and worry had left the man's voice. He spoke with strong intent. Rain continued to fall, and it glistened on his face as it reflected off the full moon and the almost sleeping sun.

A kind of roar came from the area where the two men were. It was more of a desperate shriek than a declaration of dominance. Like something was in a fight, but losing. With Dylan in her embrace, Jessica scampered back to a few steps away from Will and Samuel. Dylan cried out and buried his face into Jessica's side. He then let go of her so he could bring his hands up to his ears and cover them, and began bawling, a muffled cry of terror sinking into her shirt.

Samuel's eyes opened and he slowly lowered his head to look down to Will. Still speaking in a strange dialect, he slowly brought his outstretched hand in to clasp at his chest with the other. His strong voice went away, and he now mumbled. An uneasy feeling panned Jessica's mind, but she couldn't look away.

In an instant, Samuel went silent. When this happened, Dylan stopped crying and looked down at the two men, still hugging his chest to Jessica's side. Samuel simply stared at Will. He still held something tight at his chest, but the only sound was that of rain pattering down on the cooling asphalt.

Jessica took another few steps back, now standing on the shoulder of the road, across from Will and Samuel.

Opening his mouth wide, Samuel made a grotesque sound that startled her. It was as if he'd tried to inhale all the air around them at once, and made this painful sounding gasp in reaction. Streetlights illuminated the road, and Jessica caught a glimpse of Samuel's face. The whites in his eyes showed, pupils apparently lost somewhere in the back of his head. It looked demonic, and she wondered if she should just take the boy and run. But she couldn't.

Will's back arched violently. Stranger still, he let out a more ghostly gasp than Samuel had. Dylan started to race to Will's side, but Jessica managed to catch his collar and pull him back.

"No," she said.

Samuel spoke. This time, it was in English. Four simple words that Jessica knew she would never forget.

"Fly into me, demon."

Will's head jerked up, and his eyes were stark white, much like Samuel's. He gasped and let out a hellish scream before falling back onto the asphalt.

Jessica couldn't believe her eyes. She thought she was dreaming.

A gunmetal cloud of smoke flowed from Will's mouth. It was thick, with no particular shape or consistency. The cloud rose out of Will and flew its way into Samuel's mouth. He made a strange sound as he began to swallow the cloud, inch by inch. Some time had passed, and the tail of the cloud left Will's body, Samuel inhaling it like smoke, taking in the last little bit and closing his mouth.

Samuel's eyes closed, and he slumped over onto the concrete.

Both Will and Samuel's bodies lay still.

Jessica left the boy's side and faltered toward the two unmoving bodies. The storm had slowed, but rain still fell in scattered drops. Her hair was soaked, parted flat and straight from the downpour, and her clothes were drenched. Her eyes were on Will, trying to see if he was breathing. His stomach was flat and his eyes were closed, the skin on his face still so pale.

All the while, the young woman fought to process what she'd just seen. How was she supposed to explain to the rest of the group what had happened?

She stood over Will. It felt like she was looking directly into a coffin as he lay there with his arms crossed, similar to how you'd see those placed on the deceased. Falling to one knee, she took his hand.

"Go to them," she said. "Go to your par—"

Her words were interrupted by a horrific growl behind her. She turned just in time to see Samuel rise up into a sitting position and reach for her. His hands clasped her shoulders, and she screamed.

The eyes. Empty and pale. Samuel was one of *them*.

He worked to try and pull her toward him and she fought it off, even grasping Will's pants leg to try and gain leverage.

The beast clicked its teeth and continued to spit and snarl. Her shirt sleeve ripped, and it was almost as if this angered the creature. It bellowed louder. She felt a sharp pain on her shoulder blade as she fought her way to her feet, the creature having dug its nails into her.

There was a loud 'boom' then, and then a thud.

The beast Samuel lay flat on its back. The thud had apparently been its head smacking the concrete.

Then Jessica faced forward and saw Dylan standing a mere five yards away, a pistol drawn and exhaling smoke from its barrel.

"Dylan."

She jumped to her feet and scurried to the boy. Carefully removing the gun from his grip, she held it aside and embraced him. Dylan returned the gesture, wrapping his short arms around her.

A gasp, and then the boy pulled away. It was a terrifying sound, like someone raising their head above water just as they'd been on the verge of drowning.

She turned around.

And he was alive.

CHAPTER TWENTY-TWO

<u>Gabriel</u>

Blink.

Blink.

A haze washed over him as he opened his eyes.

Gabriel wasn't sure how long he'd been out, and as he started to come to, a familiar voice spoke to him.

"Gabriel, you okay?"

The voice belonged to Holly. She squeezed his arm.

"Wake up."

Blink.

His eyes opened wide, looking up at the slatted ceiling. His attention shifted toward Holly, who sat on her legs beside him.

"How long have I been out?"

"Not really sure," Holly said. "You ran into the house a while ago, and we started to get really worried when you never came back out. But we were pinned down and unable to come after you. Do you remember what happened?'

Gabriel sat up and felt the blood rush to his head. Holly tried to urge him to lie back down, but he wanted to try and adjust his body to being upright again. His lips were dry, and he circled them with his tongue to wet them. He tasted something on his upper lip, and brought his hand to his face. When he pulled it away, he saw the blood on his fingertips.

His nose throbbed, and he realized that's where the blood had come from.

"Hardly," Gabriel replied. "I found Dylan, but then David showed up and we got into a fight. He was going to kill me, but these two girls stopped him. That's all I remember.

Moving his hand up to a place on his head where his skull throbbed, Gabriel felt a lump. It brought back the memory of him being leveled with the butt-end of a shotgun. The blur in his vision disappeared and he was finally able to get a good look at Holly. The beautiful girl looked like she'd aged almost ten years since he'd seen her last. Blood stains rode up her arms, and spots of red were scattered on her dirt-covered face. Her eyes were bloodshot and weak.

"What happened?" Gabriel asked.

She spoke slowly, as if in shock, but she didn't falter and she didn't cry. She explained to Gabriel how they'd been in the middle of a firefight with the people who occupied this farm, when a truck came soaring at them. Will had stepped out in front of it when he saw David was driving, and fired at him. Just before David had hit Will with the truck, Marcus had pushed Will out of the way and had sacrificed himself for Will.

"I'm not even sure he felt anything," Holly mumbled.

It hit Gabriel like a brick. Marcus had become a good friend over a short period of time, and he'd sacrificed his own life for another one of their own. But there was unfortunately no time to grieve, not with others still out there.

"David had Dylan with him. Did you see him in the truck with him? And where's Will now?"

Holly looked away and stared at the adjacent wall.

"What?" Gabriel asked. "What's the matter? Are they okay?"

She looked back toward him now, but not directly at him.

"I don't know," Holly said. "Will jumped into the truck and took off after them."

Grumbling, the joints in both his knees popping, Gabriel managed himself to his feet. His back had stiffened from lying on the hardwood, but it wasn't anything that wouldn't work itself out, the longer he stood. By the time he had worked his way down the hall, to the stairs, Holly was already at the bottom, making her way over to the exit. A car door slammed outside. Holly peeked through the drapes that dressed a window next to the entrance.

"Oh my God."

Holly swung the door open and ran outside.

Holding onto the banister, Gabriel shuffled down the stairs with haste, ignoring the pain in his sciatic nerve and the lump on his head.

The front door was ajar, and when he looked out, he saw Holly running toward a vehicle. The passenger side door was open, and a small figure stepped out and looked around. Gabriel's heart thumped in his chest. He moved to the middle of the archway, then stepped out onto the old patio.

The boy turned to look toward the house, and the moon shone down enough light to show his smile.

Dylan ran to the front porch.

***

Jessica

The car door creaked as it opened. Smoke rose from the

engine, and it finally puttered out. Jessica tried to crank the pickup again, but it wouldn't turn over. She was surprised the car had started at all, to even get them back to the farm. The damage to the engine appeared to have been catastrophic after David had run the car off the road and into a tree.

No one seemed to notice that the vehicle wouldn't re-start. On the other side of the car, Holly held Will in a tight embrace, crying into his shoulder. And Dylan had run up to the house and jumped into Gabriel's arms.

Jessica was looking out toward the barn when, out of the corner of her eye, she noticed Will pulling away from Holly. Jessica turned around, and watched as Will stepped around the back side of the vehicle and walked twenty yards over to where two bodies lay on the ground.

Stepping through the tall grass, Jessica moved close enough to where she could see Marcus lying on the ground closest to him, and then a female body another five to ten yards off which appeared to be that of the nurse, Sarah. Her body had apparently fallen out of the truck when Will raced after David.

Will knelt down next to Marcus' body and grabbed his friend's hands, setting them one over another on top of his chest. It was difficult to tell what exactly had happened, though part of Marcus' mid-section appeared disfigured. Jessica knew she'd later find out what had happened, and opted not to force the subject now.

Footsteps approached from behind, ruffling in the grass, and a hand clasped Jessica's. She looked over to see Holly. The slightly shorter woman held a neutral expression on her face, her eyes and cheeks blushed from weeping, and she kept ahold of Jessica's hand and looked over to Will. Jessica didn't question her, but took the act as a form of truce-making. If they were to survive, she knew that the remaining five in the group would need to stick together, and she was grateful to see that Holly appeared to be coming to that same conclusion.

More rustling in the grass, and Jessica turned to see Gabriel and Dylan walk up beside them, the boy's small hand joined with Gabriel's.

"We have to bury them," Will said, not looking up from Marcus' corpse. "Including Samuel."

"Who?" Gabriel asked.

"The man who saved me," Will said. "His body is in the back seat of the car."

Everyone remained silent for a moment. Jessica thought to herself how she'd never seen anyone die in her life up until a week ago, and now it seemed routine. It sickened her to think she was almost immune to the look and the smell, though the sad, dark feeling of loss hadn't seemed as if it would ever go away.

"What happened to Mary Beth?" Dylan asked.

"To who?" Gabriel asked.

"The girl that the bad people took away. Is she okay?"

Gabriel looked toward the others, apparently seeking help on how to respond.

"She ran away," Will said honestly.

"But is she okay? We have to go find her!"

"We can't go find her, buddy," Gabriel said. "We don't know where she went."

The boy bowed his head, crossing his arms over his chest.

Jessica looked up and glanced over to the barn.

"I'm gonna go see if I can find a couple of shovels," she said. "You wanna come with me, Dylan?"

"I don't wanna go in there," Dylan said.

"You sure?"

The boy kept his eyes to the dirt and didn't respond.

Will finally looked up from Marcus' body.

"I need to take a walk," Will said.

"Let me go with you," Holly said.

Will shook his head. "I need to be alone." He leaned over and kissed Holly on the forehead, and walked toward the street.

Jessica looked off toward the barn and felt a hand on her shoulder.

"Take this with you," Holly said, and she handed a handgun over to Jessica.

Jessica grasped the cold grip in her hand, then acknowledged Holly.

"Holly and I will go inside and see what we can find in the way of supplies," Gabriel said. "You got the keys to the car so I can back it up to the porch, and we can just load stuff into the bed?"

"It's dead," Jessica replied. "Surprised it got us all the way back here to the farm, honestly."

"We don't have a vehicle?" Holly questioned, obvious worry in her voice.

"Dylan, you wanna come into the house with us?" Gabriel asked.

Dylan shook his head. "I don't wanna go in there either. I

just wanna go home."

Gabriel placed his hand on Dylan's shoulder. "Soon, buddy. We're going home soon. Now, come on."

"Yes, sir," Dylan said, taking Gabriel's hand.

Gabriel nodded at Jessica. Holding the gun tight in her hand, she walked toward the barn.

***

The door screamed as it swung forward on its hinges, echoing through the entire barn. Some of the light from above the outside of the door shone into the room, but it only stretched for a few feet before fading into shadows of nothingness.

A fowl smell permeated the air, and Jessica coughed.

What is that?

And the noise. Some kind of muffled noise. It didn't sound threatening, but she had difficulty making it out. The handgun became sweaty in her palm. She held the weapon tight and it nearly slipped from her grasp. What had once been cold to the touch was now damp with a nervous woman's perspiration.

Jessica reached above her head, looking for a way to turn on a light. She'd almost given up when her fingertips brushed over a thin chain and she pulled down.

The lighting came alive in the barn.

She gasped and stepped back.

There were three of them.

A trio of bodies swung from side to side in front of her, the tips of their toes just inches from brushing the scattered hay. Wrapped tightly around their necks, the chains that hung from the roof of the tall barn suspended them each less than a foot off of the ground.

They weren't dead.

Yet, also not alive.

They were Empty.

"What happened here?" Jessica said, mumbling to herself. Her breath was heavy and her heart rate had increased.

As they writhed, the three creatures continued to swing. It happened in near unison, almost like a three-piece pendulum. Two of them alternated their hands between the chains around their throats and reaching out toward Jessica. The other didn't bother with the choking hold, and instead outstretched its arms toward Jessica as if it might actually grab her. She realized that none of the things would be a threat to her, strung up the way they were, and she...

Gunshots. Four of them, all happening within seconds of each other.

The three creatures continued to swing and snarl, looking toward the rear of the barn where the gunshots had originated from. Jessica had started to turn and run out of the barn for help when a figure came out of the shadows in front of her. It was a woman with strung-out hair. Blood had splashed onto her clothes, and she held a gun squarely aimed toward Jessica.

"Drop it," the woman said, "and don't you fuckin' move."

The gun at her side, Jessica did as the woman said and dropped the gun into a collection of hay on the ground beside her.

"Now put your hands up," she demanded.

Slowly, Jessica pointed both her hands to the roof. For

having a gun aimed directly at her, Jessica had managed to remain fairly calm, so as to not show her the fear riding up inside her.

"Do you live here?" Jessica asked.

"Shut up!"

The woman took two steps toward Jessica, who jumped back a hair. The woman's eyes lit aflame, and her cheeks were flushed, too. She appeared to have been crying.

"Okay, okay," Jessica said. "Can you at least tell me your name?"

"Ah, I guess that don't matter at this point. My name's Cindy."

"Hi, Cindy," Jessica said. "Why don't you put down the gun and we can talk? I'm sure there's just a misunderstanding here."

Cindy laughed, but just as she was about to reply, her gaze fell over Jessica's shoulder and to the large entrance.

"Don't move, or I'll shoot 'er!"

"Jessica, what's going on?" Will asked.

"Put down the gun, unless you want me to drop 'er right now!"

"Don't do it, Will," Jessica said.

The crazed woman loaded a bullet into the chamber as she took two steps toward Jessica. Even with the screaming beasts hanging in the barn, the click seemed to ring inside of Jessica's head.

"Alright, I'm dropping it," Will said, and Jessica heard his weapon hit the ground.

"Now, I'll tell you what's goin' on," Cindy said. "What's goin' on is that y'all kilt my family. Now, I'ma kill all you.

One by one. Each one'a you gonna watch it."

"But, we didn't—"

"Shut the fuck up," Cindy said, cutting Will off mid-sentence. "The hell you didn't. You think I'm stupid? I saw y'all. You should've just stayed away. Got yourself in some kinda trouble now, I think. You think I won't kill y'all? Go on and look at the back of the barn. I just kilt four children."

"Oh my God," Jessica said, thinking back to the gunshots she'd heard moments earlier.

"Clint thought we could survive. That we'd be just fine in this hellhole. I wanted to take their pain away. Take them away from this miserable world. I couldn't let them continue to live here and grow up like this. They off in a better place now."

Even with the Autumn breeze, sweat glistened off of Cindy's hand under the lights. Jessica could see perspiration dancing with the freckles on the woman's cheek. She was uneasy—nervous.

"There was a man here who killed my mother," Will said. "And one of our own, a child, was kidnapped. We couldn't just stay away. I'm really sorry your family was killed; I am. I've lost both my parents over the last few days. But we can stop that trend of killing now."

Again, Cindy just laughed. "You ain't sorry for shit. Only thing you gonna be sorry about before you die is that you left me here to finish y'all off... something that idiot Clint couldn't do."

Cindy pointed the gun toward the ground. "Put your hands behind your head and get on your knees," Cindy said to Jessica.

Jessica looked down to the dirt. "Please, don't—"

A gunshot sputtered off the ground right next to her.

"Stop it!" Will demanded.

Cindy ignored him, keeping her eyes locked onto Jessica.

"On your knees, or the next bullet goes right into one of 'em."

Jessica abided, weeping more heavily now. She placed her hands behind her head and slowly lowered to her knees, one at a time. The nearest Empty swung in front of her, reaching out and trying so desperately to break free. For the first time since Melissa Kessler had urged her to keep fighting, to continue living, she wished she'd offed herself on the bed her parents had taken their own lives on. It would have been quick and painless, as opposed to having had to endure the eventual fate from the hands of a deranged backwoods woman.

Jessica looked up, ready for Cindy to press the tip of the gun against her head and pull the trigger, but it didn't happen. Instead, Cindy raised the weapon toward Will.

"Come closer," Cindy demanded.

Will made his way to the middle of the barn, leaving his gun on the ground behind him. He came forward until he was instructed to stop, which was still at a good ten feet away from Jessica. Her hands shook, and she held a tight grasp on the hair on the back of her head, as if to try and calm her nerves.

Cindy kept the gun pointed at Will, and she began to step backward. Again, Jessica had expected the woman to execute her, but she was doing something else now. Cindy walked into the shadows, and when she re-appeared, she held something in her hand.

A controller.

"I'm sorry it has to be like this," Cindy said, and she held it up and pressed down on a button.

Machinery ground and shifted above, and the Empty in the middle started to lower. Its toes touched the ground, and Jessica swore she could almost see a gleam of relief or victory in the creature's expression.

"Don't do this!" Will shouted.

Jessica screamed.

The Empty's feet hit the ground, and it took its first step toward her, the chain still restraining it for the moment. But Cindy continued to press down on the button, and with that, the beast received more and more slack from the chain with every second.

Saliva hit her face. More and more as it became closer. Behind her, she could hear Will pleading with Cindy to stop. To let her go, put him there in her stead. But none of it worked. The Empty continued to approach her, getting so close now.

Jessica closed her eyes.

She thought of her parents. Of Walt and Melissa.

I'll see you soon.

There was a different scream, a gasp, and then a type of slurping sound. Jessica looked up, and she was still just out of the Empty's reach... it had stopped. She looked behind her and saw Cindy's back facing her, but something was different.

Blood spouted from three holes in Cindy's back. Both the gun and the remote fell from her hands, hitting the ground as she turned. Jessica saw her hands clasped onto the long handle of a pitch fork. Blood pooled from her mouth. Her eyes widened and puffed, as if she wanted to cry.

Jessica covered her mouth.

A young girl, perhaps not any taller than Dylan, stood on the other side of Cindy.

Cindy slumped down onto her side, and her head slammed against the dirt as she fell.

Her eyes were vacant.

Cindy was dead.

In shock, Jessica still hadn't moved. She looked to the girl and noticed it was the same girl who'd been strapped to the table.

Will hurried over to Jessica. He took her under her arms and picked her up. She turned and hugged him, shuddering into his shoulder.

"It's okay, it's okay," Will said.

They both jumped when they heard the gunshot.

The girl stood over Cindy's body, staring down at her, the gun still pointed and her hand trembling. She looked up at Will and Jessica.

"I didn't want her to turn into one of them." She said it with a sort of apologetic innocence.

They heard someone else enter the barn, and turned to see Dylan.

"Mary Beth!" Dylan shouted, and he ran to the girl.

As he hugged Mary Beth, she cried, and clutched him back. She dropped the gun to the ground.

"It's okay," Dylan said, running his hand up and down her back.

Jessica turned when she heard others approach, and Gabriel and Holly appeared in the doorway.

"What the hell happened?" Gabriel asked.

EPILOGUE

They buried their friends in the dead of night. Every now and again, they'd hear something howl off in the distance—likely a pack of coyotes or wolves. It was a sound they all agreed they would take gladly over the guttural snarls from a horde of Empty bodies.

Before digging the holes, Will had explained to Holly and Gabriel what had happened inside the barn. He'd been surprised that neither of them had heard the gunshots from inside the house, but Gabriel had told him that the HVAC in the house had been rumbling, and the gunshots had sounded like they had come from far off in the distance; gunshots were becoming more and more common, so it hadn't even fazed them.

The three holes had been dug near the large tree where the men who owned the land had been fighting back against the group. Jessica had briefly mentioned to the others the idea of digging graves for the four children inside the barn, but when no one had responded, she didn't bring it up again. Unless someone else stumbled across this property and decided to do something about the children, they'd be left to nourish the ground inside of the barn for the rest of the time that the world turned.

Will had wanted to assist in preparing the graves, but Gabriel had insisted that he rest. In truth, Gabriel still had trouble even believing the story of Will's survival, and likely wouldn't have at all if it weren't for the bite marks not having fully healed on Will's arm. He doubted he'd even have believed that Will had been bitten by David at all if it wasn't for the torn flesh. But trying to reason that a prayer had exorcised the demon out of him? Gabriel just didn't have the faith for that.

Either way, he and the ladies could handle preparing the burial ground. Gabriel had suggested that Jessica rest, as well, having been nearly executed by a psychotic woman, but she insisted on helping, telling him that it would be more beneficial for her to do something productive rather than sit and watch him and Holly.

Dylan sat on the porch with Mary Beth, doing his best to console the young girl. He seemed to be doing fine on his own, and the adults left them alone. The boy had matured so fast.

Will had remained close by, sitting against the tree. He'd stared over at the table, now flipped over, and had wondered how many people had been put to death over the last week on it. Thankfully, they'd been able to save young Mary Beth.

Will, Gabriel, Jessica, Dylan, and Mary Beth now stood under the almost full moon, staring down into the three holes—three more innocent people vanished prematurely from their legion.

The preacher, Samuel.

Sarah.

Marcus.

Death was never easy; even in the case of someone as evil as David Ellis, it was still a human life ending. And while the group would mourn Sarah for weeks and months to come, it was especially hard for Will, Gabriel, Holly, and Dylan to say goodbye to Marcus. He'd become such an intricate part of their group, and had been a friend and co-worker of Holly's for years. Her boss, in fact, and the best one she'd ever had. Now, he was nothing but a memory.

Will was especially distraught, as two of the dead had helped him escape death. Marcus had sacrificed his own life in order to save him, diving in front of the speeding pickup truck to push him out of the way. The crash of the truck into Marcus' body was a sound that would play over in Will's mind for years to come, if he had years left in his life.

And the preacher, Samuel, had quite literally, brought Will back to life.

Will couldn't speak.

Nothing needed to be said. All five of them were exhausted, and they were tired of burying friends.

In lieu of eulogies, they stood in silence.

***

The following morning arrived, and they'd all slept until the sun began to shine through the windows. Jessica was the first to awaken. She, Holly, and Mary Beth had stayed in one of the upstairs bedrooms, while the two men and Dylan had stayed in the other. The two rooms were side by side and shared a door, so, barring their all crowding into one room, it had seemed like the safest thing to do in case someone, or something, got into the house.

Jessica stood and stared out the window as she stretched, arching her back and clasping her hands together as they reached for the ceiling. It was strange—sleeping in the house, having known the type of people who had lived there, but she was thankful just to have a real bed to sleep in. After leaving the hospital, she hadn't been sure when she'd see the luxury of a bed again.

Holly still rested in a nearby bed, lying on her side and clutching a pillow. Jessica had taken the larger bed, and Mary Beth had cuddled with her all night. The young girl still rested.

The floor creaked as Jessica crept toward the door. The hinges sounded even worse, and she was surprised the whole house didn't wake up. She shut the door behind her, and turned around just as a toilet flushed across the hall. The bathroom door swung open and Will appeared.

"Oh, good morning," Will said as he trudged out of the bathroom.

"Morning."

"How are the ladies?"

"Sleeping like babies in there. Holly's holding some dead person's pillow tight," Jessica said with a soft smile.

Will narrowed his eyes.

"Sorry," Jessica said, looking away in slight embarrassment. "That's a little weird."

Cracking a smile, Will said, "No, it's okay. In a strange way, it was kinda funny."

Part of Jessica's smile returned, and she looked back to Will.

"Do we really have to leave?" she asked.

Will nodded.

"We have everything here. Power, air and heat, a kitchen, plumbing... everything we need to survive."

"Yeah," Will whispered, "but we don't have Gabriel's wife and daughter, or Dylan's parents. And who's to say there isn't some sort of refuge, put together by the government, there?"

"Do you think there's really something like that for us there?" Jessica asked.

Will shrugged. "I have no idea. But I know there's nothing left for me here—and Gabriel already tried to go out on his own once, and we all ended up back together here. And if we had all stayed together from the beginning, my mom—"

He stopped himself mid-sentence and looked to the ground.

Turning away, he said, "I'm sorry."

Jessica thought of responding, but then the men's bedroom door opened and Gabriel exited into the hallway.

"Morning," Gabriel said.

"Excuse me," Will said, and he moved past Jessica and shuffled down the stairs, turning toward the kitchen when he reached the bottom.

Gabriel looked to Jessica and narrowed his eyes. "He okay?"

She nodded. "Yeah, just a rough couple of days. For all of us, but none more than him."

"Yeah," Gabriel mumbled.

"Is Dylan awake?" Jessica asked, changing the subject.

"Uh, yeah. He's up, but trying to actually wake up. The kid sleeps like a rock."

Jessica chuckled. "Alright, well, I'll go start waking the girls so we can try and head out soon."

"See ya downstairs."

***

Will

The sun was just starting to warm the morning when Will opened the front door and stepped out onto the patio.

Gabriel, Jessica, Holly, Dylan, and Mary Beth stood a few yards away from the bottom of the staircase, looking up at him. They'd found a couple of backpacks and duffle bags inside the house, and loaded them up with their remaining ammo, as well as some items from inside the house, including dried and canned food, and as much water as they could gather in bottles they'd found in the kitchen cabinets.

As he came down the steps, no one said anything. They each held the expressions of people who'd been through hell.

Gabriel had told him the previous night that they were just a hair under 500 miles from Alexandria, VA., where both he and Dylan lived. Will had thought about how long it had taken them to just get the 180 miles from Nashville to Knoxville, and dreaded even thinking about the journey to the East Coast.

He joined the group in the yard, though, and leaned down to give Holly a kiss. He then acknowledged Jessica and the children, sharing a nod with Gabriel lastly, who finally broke the silence.

"Hope we find a car quick," Gabriel said. "Not looking forward to walking."

"We'll find something a few miles down the road at one of those gas stations," Will said, picking up a backpack off the ground and throwing it over his shoulders.

"I hope so," Dylan said. "My legs hurt."

Smiling, Will reached over and rustled the boy's hair.

Then he turned around and took one last glance at the farmhouse.

"You know what's funny?" Will said. "I always wanted to be a farmer when I grew up."

"Well, I'm not gonna live on a farm," Holly said. "So, let's get the heck out of here."

Will stuck his thumbs under the straps on his pack and took the first step toward the main road. Footsteps followed behind him.

When he reached the three mounds of dirt in the middle of the yard, Will stopped. He drew in a deep breath, then kneeled down to Marcus' grave.

"I'll miss you, brother," Will mumbled. He set his hand on top of the mound, patted it once, then stood.

He took the two steps over to where they'd laid Samuel to rest, and squatted down once more. Will reached under his shirt, grabbing hold of the cross which he'd taken from around the preacher's neck.

"Thank you," Will whispered, rubbing the surface of the crucifix with his thumb. He rose to his feet again.

Will turned around when he heard a sniffle, and looked over to see Holly with her hand over her mouth, her eyes moist and red. He put his arm around her as Gabriel, Jessica, and Dylan said their final goodbyes; even Mary Beth took a second to say a quick prayer. Will glanced down to Holly, then continued the walk to the main road, his arm still around her.

When he and Holly reached the end of the driveway, he removed his arm from her and turned around to the rest of the group.

"Everyone ready?" Will asked.

His friends collectively acknowledged that they were.

Will nodded, then turned back around and stepped out onto the road. He hung a right toward the interstate. An Autumn morning breeze, trapped between the rows of trees on either side of the street, traveled down the path. He looked up to see the sun rearing its face over the horizon. The sky was clear, clouds of all shapes occupying its vast space. Will found himself mesmerized, no longer taking such a trivial thing as Mother Nature for granted after the recent encounter with his own death.

A hand brushed against the back of his own, then grabbed it. He looked over to see Holly smiling, her face beginning to dry and her eyes almost back to their natural color of baby blue.

He glanced back to see Jessica talking to the two children, keeping them entertained. Gabriel walked just a couple of paces behind her, scanning the area with his hands gripped firmly on the rifle.

This is my family.

Will smiled.

And then another thought came to Will.

I've always wanted to visit the nation's capital.

AFTERWORD

I sit here writing this note after fourteen hours of finishing this book in order to have it uploaded to Amazon in time to meet my pre-order deadline. I have just over an hour to spare. Yikes!

Before I go upload this, I just thought I'd take a moment to say 'thanks'. This has been an amazing and exciting year for me, and it has only been made possible by all the people —that's you—who decided to take a chance and read a brand-new author. I can't believe this is the fifth book I'm releasing this year. I'd never been able to finish a novel before this year, and now I have five books out. Wow!

I've spent hours upon hours at the keyboard this year writing these books, all while holding down a full-time job, being a husband, and a father to a now 13 month old little girl. The e-mails I get from readers and all the support makes it so much easier to wake up at 5 a.m. and work on these books before work, spend my lunch breaks writing, and take time away from my family to do what I love. Please, feel free to keep sending messages my way (info@zachbohannon.com)

Now, to the book you've just read...

If I've garnered the reaction that I was going for, you're likely still reeling from the end of this book. I'm being honest with you when I say that I'm partly terrified to go upload this manuscript to Amazon when I'm done typing this message. After talking to so many of you zombie fanatics, I know that not everyone is going to understand or appreciate my take on what an "Empty" is.

202

But the truth is, this was my idea all along. I had no desire to write another zombie book about a viral outbreak. I know that so many of you love those stories as much as I do, but I wanted to write a zombie book with my own spin, tying in my obsession with the end times as depicted in the Book of Revelation. It's by no means a religious statement; I just think Revelation one of the best horror stories of all-time!

It took me three books to get here because there was no way I could have explained "The Fall" in the first or second book without forcing it, and I couldn't be any happier about how Deliverance turned out.

Will and the gang still have a lot of story left, and I look forward to telling it to you. Book 4 will be called Open Roads and is currently in pre-production. If you want to stay up to date with its release, as well as all the other books I'm working on, please consider joining my new release mailing list at www.zachbohannon.com.

Again, thank you so much for reading.

Zach

August 21st, 2015
9:58 p.m.

P.S. (If you haven't seen The Walking Dead: Season 5, don't read this!) - I know that a big part of the storyline of the more recent episodes of The Walking Dead takes place in Alexandria. The fact that Gabriel and Dylan are from there is purely coincidental. My aunt has lived there for the past 30 or so years and I've spent a lot of time there, and I picked that city based solely on that. I had no idea Rick and his posse would end up there when I chose it. Promise.

TO BE CONTINUED...

Want to be the first to know when the next book is coming out?

Join my new release mailing list for news, exclusive content, members only giveaways and contests, and more! You'll get a free gift just for signing up.

VISIT:

www.zachbohannon.com

Zach Bohannon Books

Empty Bodies Series
Empty Bodies
Empty Bodies 2: Adaptation
Empty Bodies 3: Deliverance
Empty Bodies 4: Open Roads (coming soon)

Novels
The Witness
Lines of the Devil

Short Stories
Heritage

For a complete and up to date list
Visit Zach's Amazon Author Page at:
http://bit.ly/zachbohannonbooks

ACKNOWLEDGEMENTS

Thank you to all the readers who came across Empty Bodies on Amazon and took a chance on it.

Thank you, Kathryn, for letting me sit here for 14 hours to beat my deadline on this book, and for bringing me dinner to my office!

Thank you to The Empties!

Thanks, Johnny for another amazing cover and Jennifer for another awesome edit.

Thanks to my friends in the author community in no particular order:
J. Thorn, David J. Delaney, Dan Padavona, Richard Brown, Mat Morris, Michelle Read, Wade Finnegan, Xavier Granville, C.C. Wall, John Oakes, Simon Whistler, Robert Chazz Chute, Carl Sinclair, Darren Wearmouth, T.W. Piperbrook, J. Scott Sharp, Nancy Elliot Pertu, Sam Sisavath, Iain Rob Wright, and K.R. Griffiths.

WHAT DID YOU THINK OF *DELIVERANCE?*

For independent authors like myself, reviews are very important. You won't see my books at the grocery store or on some famous television personality's book list. Reviews help new readers discover our work so that they can enjoy our stories and we can write more books.

If you enjoyed this book, I would be forever grateful if you would take the time to click the link below and just leave a few words about what you thought about Empty Bodies 3 on Amazon. This link will take you right there:

http://bit.ly/eb3reviews

And if you have any questions or comments regarding this title, or anything else for that matter, I'd love to hear from you. Please feel free to e-mail me at info@zachbohannon.com. I personally respond to every e-mail.

ABOUT THE AUTHOR

Something about the dark side of life has always appealed to me. Whether I experience it through reading and watching horror or listening to my favorite heavy metal bands, I have been forever fascinated with the shadow of human emotion.

While in my 20's, I discovered my passion to create through playing drums in two heavy metal bands: Kerygma and Twelve Winters. While playing in Twelve Winters (a power metal band with a thrash edge fronted by my now wife Kathryn), I was able to indulge myself in my love of writing by penning the lyrics for all our music. My love of telling a story started here, as many of the songs became connected to the same concept and characters in one way or another.

Now in my 30's, my creative passion is being passed to

willing readers through the art of stories. While I have a particular fascination for real life scenarios, I also love dark fantasy. So, you'll find a little bit of everything in my stories, from zombies to serial killers, angels and demons to mindless psychopaths, and even ghosts and parallel dimensions.

My influences as a writer come primarily from the works of Clive Barker, Stephen King, and Blake Crouch in the written form; the beautifully dark, rich lyrics of Mikael Akerfeldt from the band Opeth; and an array of movies, going back to the root of my fascination at a young age with 70's and 80's slasher films such as *Halloween, Friday the 13th,* and *The Texas Chainsaw Massacre.*

I live in Nashville, Tennessee with my wife Kathryn, our daughter Haley, and our German Shepherd Guinness. When I'm not writing, I enjoy playing hockey, watching hockey and football, cycling, watching some of my favorite television shows and movies, and, of course, reading.

Connect with me online:

Website: www.zachbohannon.com
Subscribe: http://bit.ly/zbbjoin
Facebook: http://www.facebook.com/zbbwrites
Pinterest: http://www.pinterest.com/zbbwrites
Twitter: @zachbohannon32
Instagram: @zachbohannon